THE MARVELOUS ADVENTURES OF HERMAN J. ELKMOSS, MD

Jeff Jones

Best wishes!
Jeff Jones
13 Mar 08

PublishAmerica
Baltimore

© 2007 by Jeff Jones.
All rights reserved. No part of this book may be reproduced, stored in a retrieval system or transmitted in any form or by any means without the prior written permission of the publishers, except by a reviewer who may quote brief passages in a review to be printed in a newspaper, magazine or journal.

First printing

This book is a work of fiction. Names, characters, places, and incidents are products of the author's imagination or are used fictitiously. Any resemblance to actual events or locales or persons, living or dead, is entirely coincidental.

ISBN: 1-60441-003-5
PUBLISHED BY PUBLISHAMERICA, LLLP
www.publishamerica.com
Baltimore

Printed in the United States of America

Dedication

To Mrs. Herman J. Elkmoss

INTRODUCTION

The medical world was recently shocked by the untimely death of Dr. Herman J. Elkmoss. He was a prominent community leader as well as a compassionate physician, and he will be sadly missed.

The newspaper stories of his death were rather sketchy, but fortunately we have been able to interview the intern who was involved in the incident surrounding the demise of Dr. Elkmoss. The newly graduated doctor on duty that night agreed to describe what happened only under the condition of anonymity. Therefore, we will refer to him as Dr. Klutz.

Elkmoss was highly instrumental in starting up a family practice residency at Moss Community Hospital. This was its first year and there were four interns accepted into the program, Dr. Klutz being one of them. Part of their duties was to cover call in the hospital at night. In fact, one of the main reasons Dr. Elkmoss was successful in getting the residency program accepted was the service the interns provided.

One night early in the program, Dr. Elkmoss happened to be in the hospital after seeing a patient in the emergency room. A skeleton crew was on duty (the nursing shortage has made staffing the midnight shift very difficult), and as luck or bad fortune would have it, an elderly man in a private room arrested just as the night nurse was taking his vital signs. She ran out to the desk and called a code.

Dr. Elkmoss was nearby and immediately ran into the room. In his rush, he tripped and was knocked unconscious. Dr. Klutz had been down the other hall near a crash cart when he heard the code and was the next person to the room, pushing the cart. He had just heard a lecture that day about electro cardio-version, and when he saw Dr. Elkmoss on the floor, mistook him for the dying patient. Before anyone else came in, he jolted his mentor with a 400-amp charge. This put Dr. Elkmoss into cardiac arrest. When the code team made it to the room, they continued to work on Dr. Elkmoss and ignored the patient.

Dr. Elkmoss did not survive in spite of vigorous attempts by the team. Some say it was because Dr. Klutz did not intubate the mistaken patient correctly. Others felt it was just his time. As for the patient for whom the code was called? Unfortunately, he died as well.

Although cut short by this unfortunate accident, Herman J. Elkmoss's life was rich and full. He grew up in Moosetown, the home of Moss State University. Father Elkmoss was a professor at the university, and Herman earned an engineering undergraduate degree there. Herman went on to accept a fellowship in engineering in the South, but was drafted and served in the Army before he could start. After he graduated from officer candidate school and served a year at Fort South, he was sent to Vietnam. He was discharged at the end of his tour overseas and was accepted in medical school at Moss State University. After graduation he did an internship at Beach Community Hospital and then moved further south to do his residency at Southern Fungus University Medical School.

Following residency, Dr. Elkmoss returned to Swampville in his home state, about an hour's drive from Moosetown. There he went into private practice serving the area and Moss Community Hospital for more than twenty-five years before his untimely death.

In going through her husband's effects, Mrs. Elkmoss discovered many essays that he had written. She approached me to ask if I thought we could make them available to others. I knew Herman personally and it has been a great privilege to help publish them. We have put them together in a collection divided into three parts. The first one deals with medical education, the second with life as a physician, and the last is about life in general.

Mrs. Elkmoss and I both hope you enjoy *The Marvelous Adventures of Herman J. Elkmoss, MD*.

Jeff Jones

SECTION I
MEDICAL EDUCATION

Study hard and prepare yourself. One day your opportunity will come.

Father Elkmoss

CHAPTER 1
FAMILY DOCTOR

Although he did not directly influence my decision to go to medical school, our family physician, Dr. George Ralph Moosemoss, provided an early exposure to the practice of medicine and I consider him a very important part of my premedical education. Dr. Ralph, as Mother Elkmoss called him, lived only two blocks away from our house. We did not have many neighbors at that time, and a playing field (the only level place in Moosetown) stood between his house and ours. I never really saw the inside of Dr. Ralph's office until needing a routine high school sports physical as a teenager. If anyone in the family, particularly Sister Elkmoss or me, got sick, Dr. Moosemoss would just stop by the house in the evening on his way home and tend to us. If we needed a shot of penicillin (that was practically the only antibiotic available at the time), he would boil the needle and glass syringe on our stove while catching up on neighborhood activities with my parents. Sometimes he would just give us sugar pills he always carried in his alligator doctor bag. It was my first experience with what I would later learn was the placebo effect.

When I was three, I saw my first minor league baseball game and noticed how close catchers squatted behind the batters. Naturally that evening while playing in the field between the Moosemoss house and ours, I assumed the close position behind the batter. My best friend, Danny, promptly clunked me on the noggin. My parents dragged me with my bleeding head to Dr. Ralph's house. There, on a leather couch in his den (one of the only two times I was actually in his house), he put three stitches in my head. The laceration was in such a location that to keep the bandage on, he had to wrap my whole head. It was very embarrassing to walk around for about a week with a white skullcap. (Well, it started out being white. A three-year-old active kid just cannot keep his head clean for a week.)

At age six or so, Danny and I were climbing the forbidden trees behind the Moosemoss house. I grabbed a dead branch and fell backward more than twelve feet, landing in a safe position—on my head! Danny ran away and left me to wander home in a daze. (He later explained that he thought I had died and was afraid he would be arrested for murder. We were never very close after that.) My parents immediately knew something was wrong when I wanted to take a nap. After finding him at home, they took me to Dr. Moosemoss's house. He persistently and patiently questioned me. After a while, I eventually remembered where I had fallen, but was afraid to answer. I finally admitted that I had been climbing in *his* trees. Instead of the usual expected anger, both parents were relieved. That is not the way I recommend getting out of punishment for violating family rules, but it worked in this case.

Dr. Ralph had two children, Mary and George. Mary was perhaps fifteen years older than me. She married an Army sergeant at a young age and divorced him just before she had a baby. At the time, divorce was extremely rare and it generated many questions from a naive ten-year-old boy. One day as Mother Elkmoss and I drove past Mary's apartment, I started asking questions as to why I had always been told that both a husband and wife were necessary to have babies? Mary had a baby, and there did not seem to be a father around. This led to more questions, and the answers formed the basis of my education about the "birds and the bees."

When I was twelve, I inherited George's basketball backboard when he went away to college. His father and grandfather had been admired physicians in the community, and he very much wanted to carry on the family tradition. Unfortunately, George failed to get into medical school after several attempts. Eventually he earned a PhD in biology and became a highly respected professor at an Ivy League school. If I had any skills in basketball, I attribute them to practicing with his backboard. I also learned that acceptance to medical school was based not so much on who the applicant's parents were, but on who the applicant was. Most importantly, I appreciated that success can come in many areas, not just medicine.

I was a third-year medical student when practically the whole town turned out to celebrate Dr. Ralph's fifty years of practice. It was a wonderful experience to hear him discuss practicing medicine in the 1920s. Diseases such as typhoid fever, polio, and TB that we studied in medical school, but never actually treated, were common disorders when he started practice. Regardless of all the impediments in practicing medicine today such as the high costs, managed care restrictions, or malpractice issues, we really do take much better care of our patients. When Dr. Ralph first practiced there were not MRI scans to help diagnose disease, coronary artery bypass procedures to treat heart problems, or even antibiotics to cure infections. We tend to take all this and a lot more for granted, but Dr. Ralph did not.

Six months after his fifty-year practice party, Dr. Ralph retired. He seemed like a lost person then and shortly afterward, at age seventy-eight, he died. He left quite a legacy—a model of what a physician should be, an appreciation of the advances in medicine, and several valuable general lessons in life for me.

In cleaning out his office on retirement, Dr. Ralph gave me his alligator bag and some of the old instruments including the glass syringe and needles he probably had used treating Sister Elkmoss and me. When I was newly married and Mrs. Elkmoss first saw that old equipment, she accused me of being a packrat and wanted to throw it all out. I stubbornly resisted and I think she now understands why.

CHAPTER 2
PRE-MED EDUCATION

I am occasionally asked by high school students what I think is the best undergraduate program to prepare for medical school. Well, there actually have been only a couple students who have asked me that question. One was just making small talk at a party his parents were giving, and he really did not want to be there. Not only that, I am probably the worst person to ask. When I went to undergraduate school, I had no idea I would eventually end up studying medicine. I started out wanting to be an engineer.

The engineering program was a rigorous course and most of us had enough to do just to pass, let alone think about higher education such as medical school. While some of my classmates had fun jobs in the summers working in their hometowns as lifeguards and such, I even got a job in a plant to try to get a first-hand look at what engineers did.

By the summer between my junior and senior year, I worked as an engineer and actually got to do a research project for the company. This turned out to be a very rewarding experience. I was directed by a clever engineer and had extensive help in writing up the project. It was eventually published in the company's literature and may still be in their archives (but I think the company is now defunct).

When I got back to school that fall, the paper still needed more work and one of my professors allowed me to take a special research course for a much-needed "A" during the first semester of the senior year. By the time the second semester of my senior year rolled around, I was in great shape.

All through school I maintained a consistent pattern of getting better than a 3.0 (out of 4 points) average the first semesters. During the second semesters, due to a combination of increased extracurricular activities, sunshine, and a general lack of interest in studying, my grades dropped significantly. Every second semester, I had resolved to do better. I had improved, but not quite enough to get a 3.0.

I looked forward to the second semester of my senior year because, not only would I be graduating, it would be my easiest. I had only a nine-hour block engineering course that was an easy "B" and a technical English course. Ninety percent of the grade for the class was determined by a technical writing paper. Since I had the ideal paper already written from my research the previous summer, I was set for my first "B+" second semester.

The technical writing course went as expected with a few spelling tests throughout the semester. The company where I worked had edited the paper for content and grammar, and the engineering professor who had monitored the first semester research class for me carefully checked it over as well. As far as I was concerned, the paper was perfect.

On the last day of the class, the English professor came in and gave one last spelling test. When we turned in the tests, she handed back our technical writing projects. I was one of the first people done, so I eagerly got my paper and returned to my desk to gloat. You can imagine the shock when I looked down at the grade. The professor had given me a "C" for grammar, and a "D" for content!

I jumped out of my seat and rushed back for an explanation. She pointed out that the format I used, the company's, was different, so she could only give me a "C" even though there were no grammatical mistakes. As for the "D" for content? She thought the paper was too technical for her.

"What's the name of this course, lady?" I yelled. "It's called TECHNICAL WRITING!"

By that time, the professor had withdrawn into her shell of ignorance. I ended up with a "C" for the course and only achieved a 2.9 average for the semester. As a consolation, however, I did get invited to an annual engineering conclave where students from all over the country presented papers. I went with a couple folks from the class behind us, and one was a fellow named Kildeer whom I got to know better at the meeting. My "D" paper finished third in the country.

The technical writing course notwithstanding, I really enjoyed the rigorous engineering program and if I had not been drafted, I would have continued an engineering career in graduate school that fall. By the time I got out of the service three years later, however, I was worried I had forgotten everything I had learned and was fortunate to get accepted into medical school. As I walked up a big hill to the first day of class in medical school, I recognized Kildeer, also starting in medicine. As we climbed the steps we caught up on things. After finishing his last year as an undergraduate and spending two more years in graduate school, he decided to go to medical school.

So when an unsuspecting high school student asks me what he or she should take in college in preparation for medical school, I am usually vague with my answer. I tell them that it is unlikely their view of careers or life in general will be the same after four years of undergraduate school and that they need to keep that in mind as they tackle plans for college.

CHAPTER 3
ACCEPTED

Future medical students often receive their acceptance letters with great enthusiasm. That excitement is usually matched and sometimes exceeded by families, especially mothers (my-son-the-doctor syndrome). For me, however, that letter was met with a little indecision.

I have a deep dark secret that I have kept for many years. I really wanted to be a lawyer. There, I have said it, but let me explain.

In tenth grade when our class had to write a career paper, I chose the legal profession. My memory is a little fuzzy about the sequence of things, but I believe the paper was due towards the end of the first semester. Sister Elkmoss, two years ahead of me, had the same English course and warned me that the paper would be worth probably half of my grade, so I went about gathering information during the summer. I visited the university library and wrote letters requesting information from practically every law school in the country.

Besides having an easy time getting an "A" in English, I had the added joy of receiving many letters all summer long when law schools were more than eager to send me admission information. (I may have neglected to mention my age when requesting information.) For a fifteen-year-old fellow, I was thrilled to get more mail than my parents. Mother Elkmoss used to tell the story of receiving a letter of information about a law school addressed to me the same day as I graduated from medical school nearly fifteen years later.

In undergraduate school, I majored in engineering as I had a strong aptitude in math and science and thought that would best suit me. Besides, engineering students did not have to take foreign languages that I detested. I picked chemical because it was the only engineering program that did not require mechanical drawing or biology. I learned in ninth grade my ineptitude in drawing, mechanical or otherwise. I liked biology, but could not stand the tedious laboratory hours. So I picked chemical engineering.

I still had law on my mind when I graduated from undergraduate school, but I did enjoy chemical engineering. Therefore, I took the LSAT and GRE and applied to three graduate schools in chemical engineering and three law schools. I got accepted to Moss State and Rocky State University Law Schools along with the three graduate schools. All the graduate schools offered fellowships that would pay tuition as well as a stipend that would have been welcomed by a destitute student such as me. In the end, money ruled. I could not see how I could afford law school and accepted one of the fellowships in engineering. I then went to work as an engineer during the summer before starting the master's degree program.

At the end of summer, I packed up from the job to move into an apartment and start my fellowship. When I checked the mailbox one last time, there was a letter with a draft notice. Instead of driving to graduate school, I went home, unpacked, and a week later was inducted into the service with literally just the clothes I was wearing and a shaving kit.

Less than two years later, I was on orders for Vietnam, knowing that when (and if) I returned, I wanted to go back to school. Since I would have the GI Bill to help, I thought I could finally go to law school. When I reapplied, however, they told me I had to take the

LSAT again as it was more than three years since I took it the first time. The test was administered near Fort South where I was stationed, and the following day, they were administering the MCAT exam as well. I had always been good at taking tests and I liked having options, so I signed up for both exams. After all, my commanding officer gave me the two days off without charging me leave time.

I reapplied to Rocky State and Moss State University Law Schools and three medical schools including Moss State. On my way back from Fort South, I interviewed the medical schools. Since Moss State University Medical School was in my hometown, I saved it for last. Professors were hard to find towards the end of the summer as most were on vacation, so one of my interviews had two candidates at the same time. During the discussion, the professor asked the other student, Bill, how long he had wanted to become a physician. Bill thought he wanted to be a doctor since he was about seven years old. The professor turned and asked me.

Without hesitating I said, "When I was seven, I think I wanted to be a cowboy."

Both the professor and I laughed, but Bill did not. Both of us were eventually accepted, but I do not think he spoke to me the entire four years of medical school.

At the end of the summer, I shipped out to Vietnam with applications for law and medical schools complete. One of the ways a soldier keeps his sanity is the expectation of coming home and a future life, so for the first half of my duty in Vietnam, I was happy just "expecting to be accepted." By the following February, however, I had heard nothing. When Father Elkmoss checked, he found that I had been reaccepted at Rocky State. Moss State University Law School, my hometown undergraduate university that had accepted me three years earlier, rejected my application. Interestingly, while two medical schools and Moss State University Law School outright turned me down, Moss State University Medical School put me on an alternate acceptance list. (Seems that they were disturbed that I had no biology in undergraduate school.)

At the end of the summer after returning from Vietnam and leaving the service, I packed my car to start law school at Rocky State University. I checked my mailbox one more time and in it was my acceptance to Moss State University Medical School. I was a little perplexed with the news, but after a couple minutes at our kitchen table, I called Moss State to tell them I accepted. I sent a letter to Rocky State University Law School to thank them, but declined their offer.

With medical legal issues continuing to plague the practice of medicine, some physicians have gone on to earn a law degree. I even had some of those thoughts many years ago. In reality, though, I have truly enjoyed the profession and have never really regretted the decision to go to medical school.

CHAPTER 4
MY SON THE DOCTOR

Mother Elkmoss was arguably the proudest Elkmoss of the family when her son was accepted into medical school. She was also well aware of obnoxious mothers who constantly brag about their children and was determined not to become one of those types. I could see her resisting the temptation of boasting about me when meeting new people at parties and saying something like, "Hi, my name is Mrs. Elkmoss. Did you know my son has been accepted in medical school?"

Even before starting medical school, I could see she needed some sort of incentive, so I made her a promise. If she could avoid using the term, "My son the doctor," I would give her a copy of the very first prescription I would write as a licensed physician. That helped slow her down some until the day I graduated from medical school.

Father Elkmoss was a professor in the engineering school at Moss State University. He only had a master's degree, but that was fairly common in the 1940s, especially for engineers, when he first joined the faculty. One of his more pompous students was a certain William Benn. Billy, as we referred to him in our house, struggled through the undergraduate program, then took several extra years getting his master's degree. Finally, after several more years he obtained a PhD in engineering. Generally such dogged determinism to get through a program was something Mother Elkmoss would have applauded, but Billy seemed to be gloating over his new degree. That, in her eyes, was a big detraction.

Once Billy received his PhD, he insisted everyone call him "Doctor." At his reception in the department celebrating the event, Mother Elkmoss came up to him and said, "Congratulations, Billy, I know you really worked hard."

"Thanks," he said, "I'd like to be called Doctor Benn from now on."

Mother Elkmoss was fairly quick witted, so she immediately retorted, "Oh, *Doctor* Billy, you've taken so long to get through the program that it will take me a little while to get used to your new title."

Dr. Billy stayed on the faculty and, unfortunately, I had to put up with him as an undergraduate. When I was finishing, I applied to Moss State University's graduate engineering program. By that time, Billy was on the selections committee (usually a job given to the low man in the department), and he interviewed me. In a pompous manner he told me that there were two kinds of graduate students—those who were superstar engineers and "B" students who would just get by. (I knew what kind he was.) He said, "Unfortunately, you will be the latter."

When I told my parents about Billy's observations, Father Elkmoss just laughed (which was rare for him), but Mother Elkmoss became silent (also rare for her). You could mess with her husband and even insult her, but if you harmed a hair of her offspring, she became like a mother bear. She never said anything more about it, but I could tell she was waiting for revenge.

I subsequently accepted a graduate school fellowship at another university, but was drafted in the service before beginning. After separating from the service, I was accepted to medical school at Moss State. Sadly Father Elkmoss died of a heart attack just after my return from overseas. Mother Elkmoss, in the meantime, had gone back to school and earned a bachelor's degree in biology and a master's degree in journalism. She was teaching technical writing in the engineering school when Professor Elkmoss died and then later became assistant to the dean of engineering. While I was in medical school, she was in charge of scheduling and planning all the conferences for the engineering school, including having to work with Billy Benn. He ran seminars for the chemical engineering section (another assignment usually reserved for the low man in the department).

On graduation day from medical school, I stopped by the engineering school to give Mother Elkmoss some tickets. As luck would have it, Billy Benn was in her office at the time, going over plans for an upcoming seminar. She explained that she would not be able to help him that afternoon as she was going to attend the graduation ceremony of her son from medical school. With glee in her eye she proudly said, "You remember Herman, don't you? This is MY SON THE DOCTOR! He's the one you tried to discourage from graduate school."

In spite of this blatant use of my-son-the-doctor term, Mother Elkmoss actually did get a copy of the first prescription I wrote as a physician. When I started my internship at Beach Community Hospital, the first night I pulled duty in the emergency room and it was there that I wrote my first official script. I preserved a copy. Several years later, as Mother Elkmoss was dying from lymphoma, I wrapped it up in a get-well card. In the midst of the sorrow of losing the battle with cancer, a big smile came over her as she opened the card.

The first patient I had seen in the ER had come there because she had run out of pills and could not get in touch with her family doctor. When I called her physician, he said, "Oh, just fill out a prescription for her." The first prescription I had written as a licensed physician turned out to be for birth control pills!

CHAPTER 5
GRANDPA

Although Mother Elkmoss was by far the most excited about my acceptance in medical school, Grandpa was quite proud as well. Some of that pride probably stemmed from his very poor beginnings and the joy of having a grandchild reaching a high level of success.

He was born in the late 1800s in a farmhouse that literally had a dirt floor. He was the oldest of seven children and very bright, with aspirations of going to medical school. When his mother died at an early age, however, Grandpa had to help raise the rest of the family and gave up higher education in favor of a successful job as a salesman. He married early and was one of the rare individuals that kept his job through the Great Depression in the 1930s. As a salesman, he was always well dressed or what he referred to as "presentable." While he was not a heavy drinker, in his line of work he had his share of alcohol and was particularly fond of Michelob beer.

He was also an opinionated man (I can never remember him referring to Roosevelt without the prefix "damn") and had a very strong and favorable opinion about me. Perhaps I represented the son he never had, and serving in Vietnam (he was very patriotic) was important to him as well. Then too, it might have been the vicarious thrill of having a grandson in medical school. Whatever the reason, Grandpa and I had a special affinity towards each other. In looking back at our relationship, I can see several influences he had on me.

When I was nine or ten years old, Grandpa developed a bowel obstruction, sepsis, gangrene, and almost died. During the prolonged hospitalization of almost eighty days, our family frequently visited with him. It was the first time I had been in a hospital.

As a result of this catastrophic illness, Grandpa had a permanent colostomy. It was a distinct blow to this proud man who placed a lot of importance on independence and appearance, but I saw him adjust and deal with the new situation in a straightforward manner. Because alcohol would cause the colostomy to run uncontrollably, he had to give up drinking beer altogether. One day while lamenting the inability to appreciate a Michelob, Grandpa said, "Well, Herman, if I never have another beer, it won't be like I haven't had my share." It is a philosophy that applies to many things in life—to fully appreciate what you have now!

Another important lesson Grandpa passed on to me came during my second year of medical school. In the first year of school, we were generally taught basic sciences. The second year focused on pathological states, but we had very little experience in clinical medicine or actually dealing with people. That would start in the third year.

When Grandpa turned eighty, he explained that he had become an octogenarian, a term popularized by Ben Franklin who was a favorite of his. One day while I was visiting, Grandpa noticed a blotch under his skin on the back of his hand.

"Say, Herman," he said, "you're in medical school now. What is this?"

I looked at it and proudly said, "I think they call that senile ecchymosis, Grandpa!"

Not noticing the steam rising from Grandpa (after all, I was just looking at the hand), I went on. "As you get older, the skin gets thinner and you can easily injure yourself."

Grandpa was beside himself. "I am not senile, young man! You better pay more attention in class if you expect to graduate."

And that was the end of talking with Grandpa that day.

The following year, when I was a third-year medical student, Grandpa had developed prostate cancer. As it metastasized, the doctors instituted more treatments. Towards the end when he was in the hospital after surgery, I visited the proud man. He was having a great deal of difficulty moving around, but still tried to be presentable.

"How are you doing, Grandpa?" I asked as I helped my very tired and painful grandfather out of bed.

"Well, Herman," he said as he slowly walked to the hallway, "I'm kicking my heels, but not raising much dust."

Grandpa lived for another couple months, but finally died in his own bed at age eighty-one. His extended family met at the funeral home and shared stories of his life. One incident happened when I was born. Mother Elkmoss had prolonged labor, and Grandpa endured the wait by sitting in a bar. He had beer on his breath when he went to see his daughter after the delivery. All the pains of labor were visited on Grandpa by the rest of the family because of his drunken state at such an important time.

At the funeral home that evening, someone pointed out that there was a bar with Michelob on tap just across the street. The family quickly adjourned and gathered at the pub for one last tribute. It was more a festive occasion, just like he had always wanted at his funeral, when the family drank a beer and toasted, "This one's for you, Grandpa!"

CHAPTER 6
CADAVERS

As part of a program to develop a new alumni newsletter, Moss State University Medical School put a call out to former graduates for stories to pass along to medical students. One of the earliest traumatic events in a budding student doctor's life is his or her first look at a cadaver, so I thought I would write about my experience. On further reflection, however, I did not send them the story. The newsletter would probably have enough material on the topic, and they suffered enough by putting up with me for four years. Why torture them further?

My first look at a cadaver was certainly different than what my family physician, Dr. Moosemoss, had experienced. He described the event, more than fifty years earlier, at his medical school when each student had to blindly reach down in a vat of formaldehyde containing preserved bodies and pull out a dead body. His cadaver was a relatively young person who had been hanged! Moosemoss and his fellow students spent many hours in the dissecting lab looking at the stretch marks and trying to figure out what heinous offense their cadaver had committed. That might seem a little disgusting, but his cadaver, being so young, was the best in the class.

On the other hand, I slowly opened the metal doors covering our dissecting table to see a brown, shrunken old lady. I stood there with the other three students I would be sharing the body with for the next two years, feeling a little lightheaded. The formaldehyde fumes did not help, but the anticipated jeers of fellow classmates kept me from fainting.

Our combined intelligence did not help us find certain parts of this lady's anatomy that had shriveled up. Later to our delight, though, we discovered a brain tumor. All the other members of our class pressed in closely to see it. The instructor even marked it on an exam and gave us extra credit if we had enough sense to know it was probably a benign meningoma.

After the first traumatic day of opening our tables, serious learning took place. We quickly learned to wear old clothes to the lab, as it was impossible to avoid getting saturated with formaldehyde. Many budding doctors named their cadavers and they generally exercised considerable originality. For the sake of the cadavers' dignity (certainly not of my fellow students), I will not elaborate on those names. Typical practical jokes were kept to a minimum, but a couple students could not help sneaking pieces of cold roast beef in the canister on the dissecting table that was used to hold body parts for disposal. They then ate pieces of meat from the plastic box while standing in front of some of their colleagues. One med student was so disgusted that he passed out, striking his head on a table and sustaining a sizable, bloody laceration. Considering most of us were on edge already with all those dead people around, the experience quickly put an end to such shenanigans. Unfortunately, other classes did not get the message.

Dental students also had cadavers to study, although I hope they do not have to do that now. I have a problem knowing that a dentist, while working on my teeth, has extensive knowledge of how to find my appendix.

One of the dental classes was working late one evening, studying for an exam on the GI system. None of the faculty was around and students tend to get a little punchy at times like that. One student cut out his cadaver's small intestine and skipped rope with it. Such an event would not have been noteworthy except that this aspiring tooth fairy had a roommate that was in journalism. And having a journalism roommate usually would not have been a problem, but the budding writer had to get an article turned in for the school newspaper the following morning. Out of desperation, he wrote an exposé on anatomy classes and used the example of skipping rope with a cadaver's intestine.

A school newspaper is an interesting educational tool. While it functions as a training program for young journalists, it also is supposed to showcase the university. As a quality school news vehicle, it was sent around the state to various alumni as a marketing device. One such benefit was that when an old alumnus would die, he or she might want to leave something to posterity. If they did not have any qualms about people cutting on their corpses, they could leave their bodies to the medical school. A medical school is always in need of more cadavers, and Moss State University Medical School was as needy as any. Hence, instead of every student (including dental students) having a body, each cadaver had four goons working on it.

When the president of the university saw the article about students jumping rope with cadaver intestines, he went ballistic. The dean of the medical school (a tenuous job at best) and the dean of journalism school were in deep trouble. This transferred down to the students involved. As far as I know, the dental student, after suffering untold punishment, changed majors to criminology and is still writing a book on prison reform. You would think his journalism buddy was the only one to escape serious repercussions, but I think part of the dental student's castigation was for certain acts of retribution towards his roommate.

These incidents provided a certain sobering quality to our anatomy class, so the remainder of our two years was relatively benign. One can easily see, however, that I was not accurate when I said I wanted to spare medical students from my old school the torture of this story. In reality, I am afraid of the repercussions such an exposé would have.

CHAPTER 7
HOSPITALS

I usually tell folks that the first time I had ever been in a hospital was between my first and second year in medical school when Kildeer, a fellow classmate, and I spent the summer pushing gurney and wheelchair patients to and from a radiology department at a hospital on a beach in the South. That really is not true. I had, in fact, seen a couple of hospitals before.

When I was nine or ten years old, my grandfather had developed a bowel obstruction and then gangrene, almost dying during a prolonged hospitalization of seventy-nine days. I know the number of days well as he was a tough old bird and for the remainder of his life into his eighties, he often reminded his impressionable grandchildren of his close and prolonged brush with death.

What I would call my first real exposure to a hospital happened while I was in the service and stationed at Fort South. It was during the Vietnam War and just a couple years before a more modern hospital was built on the post. After seeing and experiencing military medicine, it is a wonder that I ever would have considered a medical career. Perhaps it helped understanding that military and civilian reasoning are quite different.

Towards the end of my year at Fort South, the commanding officer of my section, a drunk, wrapped his car around a southern pine tree. There is a saying that God takes care of fools (thus accounting for my good life) and drunks. In my chief's case, the Lord had to work overtime. The commander's car was totally destroyed along with the pine tree, but the only injury he sustained was a dislocated shoulder.

The commander's office was staffed with all majors except a lowly lieutenant—me. No one liked the chief, but they knew someone from the office had to make a call to express our sympathies (at least for the pine tree involved in the accident). Naturally, the duty fell on the kicking-boy of the office. The one concession I got was that I could get out of the office early and have the rest of the day off.

The hospital was near the officer's billets where I stayed, so it was not hard to figure out how to get there. The trouble was that the old World War II hospital was spread out all over the place. It was a one story wooden structure with many corridors attaching bays of ten to twenty beds. One of the majors explained that when it was designed, TB and other communicable diseases were running rampant. In those days they did not have effective antibiotic treatment like they have now. To avoid spreading hard-to-control diseases, patients would be segregated in different areas. Thus, there were miles and miles of halls connecting many little alcoves.

I finally found the colonel and dutifully extended the office's condolences. I always felt uneasy around my chief. I think it had to do with him wanting me to be his protégé or something when I had little respect for him.

The bay next to the orthopedic unit was the radiology department. That makes sense. The patients needing the most x-rays are orthopedic patients, so having them near radiology is logical. As I left the orthopedic bay, I heard yelling and screaming. A rather heavy lady had undergone a barium enema. The bathroom was located down the long hallway from the x-ray suite, and after the procedure, she was instructed by the technicians to hold her cheeks together and go to the bathroom. Unfortunately, she misunderstood what "cheeks" they were talking about. I was greeted by this poor lady, wearing a robot type gown open in the back, holding her face and expelling barium behind her while being chased by three technicians!

The colonel recovered and was replaced by a more sober chief, I was sent to Vietnam, and the old World War II hospital was replaced by a modern hospital. I guess it all ended up for the best.

CHAPTER 8
HERB NOTES

When I started medical school, I expected it to be grueling, and like most of my classmates, I resolved to keep up with assignments. For the first six or eight weeks, I dutifully went to the library and studied for hours on hours. Regardless of the number of times I read the anatomy text, though, it just did not make any sense. In retrospect, I wished I had spent more time discussing the subjects with my classmates and paying better attention to our excellent instructors. How the material was presented was very important to my understanding.

As we gathered in the library to study for the first set of exams and were furiously reading the incomprehensible textbooks and meager notes, someone noticed that one of our classmates, Herb, reading well-written, typed papers. For each class he had taken excellent shorthand notes and then typed out the complete lecture that evening. He thought it was a good way to review the day's lesson. It was quite simple, then, for him to review the notes before a test. Considering the uselessness of reading the textbook, we all had to agree.

Someone was smart enough to ask Herb if he would copy his notes for the whole class. Herb agreed and for twenty dollars, most of our class of eighty-five students had a complete copy of all the lectures for the semester. Herb did little more than usual and collected about $1,500. For the rest of the class, though, he was a lifesaver.

During the first two years, then, our class sat back and gave the lecturers full, undivided attention. Disaster awaited us, however. Just like birds that get reliant on folks feeding them in the winter and get in trouble if the supply stops, our class became dependent on Herb notes.

Besides being a very well organized person and an accomplished scribe, Herb was also a former pilot in the Air Force. In November of the first year, he flew some friends to Canada to hunt moose. By taking most of the trip during Thanksgiving vacation, he actually missed only three lecture days. But, oh, those three days!

Unaccustomed to taking notes and highly dependent on them, the class held an emergency meeting. They agreed that six of the best note takers would work in teams to record each lecture while Herb was gone. Herb, for his part, promised to type the notes and even bring back everyone some moose meat if he actually shot one. Even with that deal, Herb received anonymous hate mail. Actually, I think a few students were just ticked that he did not have enough room in the plane for them to go along.

Herb and his buddies were successful in shooting a moose, but because of weight restrictions in their small plane, they could only bring back several moose steaks—not enough to feed the class. To avoid a riot (after all, we were just getting over a traumatic experience of no Herb notes), he wisely decided to keep the meat for himself.

The class made it through this harrowing experience, but provisions were made in Herb's "contract" for the second semester stipulating that he could not have any absences. There was also one unexpected reaction to the whole affair. While the medical school class was highly talented and competitive, they had to work together to make up for Herb's absence and they became much more collegial. In addition, they experienced a certain vicarious thrill seeing a fellow classmate like Herb go off in the middle of a school year and hunt moose.

CHAPTER 9
MOTORCYCLE MINDY

Although our medical school class of eighty-five had common interests in medicine and learning, they also had a variety of backgrounds. There was a former Air Force pilot, a Navy lieutenant, and an Army Vietnam veteran (me). Some had attended Ivy League schools, and one guy, Rock, had been a true beach bum. One of the most unique students, however, was Mindy. She had graduated from college and joined a motorcycle gang for a couple of years. She actually drove to medical school with her gang, riding a Harley, and thus obtained her nickname—Motorcycle Mindy.

Melinda, her given name, was blond-haired, carried a little too much weight, but had a pleasant smile and ready laugh. She was obviously very smart, but her reasons for wanting to go to medical school remained obscure. It was a time when women were getting more active in achieving equality and asserting themselves, but Mindy did not seem the type wanting to make a statement. In looking back, perhaps the most likely explanation for Mindy applying to medical school was because she genuinely liked people and she could do it. Nike shoes had not been invented yet.

During the first two years, most of the work was classroom style with a series of lectures followed by formal written tests. Mindy, with her high intelligence, was very comfortable with this and tended to stay by herself. In a way, this self-sufficiency may have led to her downfall. When medical students had difficulty with certain subjects, they usually got together with others who could help. This provided a support system for rough times—and there were certainly rough times for almost everyone. Mindy, because she was so competent, never developed that support system, and when a calamity occurred, she did not have enough help. The crisis for Mindy came at the same time when many medical students had them—at the start of the third year with clinical rotations.

Mindy was in our group of five students. Most groups had six people in them, but ours was a little short of manpower so to speak. After a relative easy six-week rotation in outpatient clinics, we began our first in-patient service with psychiatry. I was on call the first evening and got pulled out of the orientation to go to the emergency room and see a patient who thought he was Jesus. It took several hours for me to take care of the patient and several more hours to write it all up. There is a great deal of criticism of doctors' handwriting, but you can begin to see how mine deteriorated after writing more than seven pages of notes on patients like that. With several other admissions to deal with, I never did get caught up with our group for a proper orientation.

The following day, my buddy Kildeer took call and suffered similar problems. At midnight the second evening, I was sitting in the workroom with him, finishing the paperwork on my fourth admission from the day before and looking forward to getting some sleep at last. Kildeer was finishing his second admission for the day. He still had another workup to do when the ER called about a possible admission.

"I'm just not going to make it," Kildeer said. "I can't handle this."

I was worn out, but I did not like the look of my tired buddy and offered to go to the emergency room for the new patient. Secretly I thought there might be a chance that the patient did not really need admission and I could skate off to bed. That was not the case.

At 5 a.m., Kildeer and I ate breakfast together in the cafeteria. At least it was free. It was the worse time of his career, but he survived and it gave both of us an inner strength that carried us through the rest of medical school. We knew we could handle just about anything after that experience.

The following day, Motorcycle Mindy pulled call, but when she had a similar experience to Kildeer's, there was no one there to help. She became progressively depressed during the rotation and while most of the melancholic patients we cared for improved, she did not.

At the end of the rotation, Mindy was so depressed with medical school she dropped out and eventually enrolled in a rehabilitation program provided by the school for such problems. Besides the tragedy of the potential loss of a talented person in medicine, our group shrank and we were on call every four nights instead of five.

Sometime during Mindy's rehabilitation she underwent a religious conversion. She eventually returned to medical school and insisted on being called Melinda. She also collected an entourage of nursing students that participated in extensive cult rituals. The group apparently felt they had the power to save patients by divine intervention.

One night while on cardiology service, Melinda and several other nursing students dressed up in white robes, lit candles and incense, and gathered around a comatose man in the cardiac unit. At about 2 a.m., surrounded with these students chanting incantations, he woke up. Thinking he had died, the patient started screaming and pulled off his EKG leads. This activated an alarm and the cardiac arrest team came charging into the unit only to see all the nursing students holding candles and standing around this petrified man. I was not there, but I am told they are still telling stories about the incident some thirty years later. It had to have been quite an event.

Melinda returned to counseling and her rehabilitation program. By the time she finally returned to medical school, we had all graduated, so I never did find out what happened to her. Considering the uniqueness of Mindy, though, I'm sure she is doing something quite unusual.

CHAPTER 10
MED STUDENT PARTIES

Several years ago at a medical education conference, one of the attendees pointed out that student doctors tend to learn as much from fellow classmates as they do from their professors. As I look back at my medical education, I can see a lot of truth in that. We tended to learn a lot from next-door neighbors as well.

As a medical student, however, I still thought that teachers were responsible for all the teaching, and the students were responsible to learn just what they were taught—the corollary to "teaching to the test" was "learning for the test." That served well enough in undergraduate school. I would find out that there was much more to learn in medical school than just what was taught in the classroom.

By the end of the first semester in medical school, our class had started to come together. We shared class notes, helped each other study, and partied together to celebrate grueling tests. Harry, one of the few married classmates, decided to have a Christmas party at his house. Most of us medical students were single and brought dates, but there was also another married couple, Tom and his wife, Tammi.

One of the first practical things we learned in psychiatry was that any party with a drunk and a hysteric would be very exciting. Tammi fit the bill as a hysteric. She was blond, flirted with everyone, and generally was the life of any party. By then, all us med students were familiar with her behavior, so it really was a lot of fun to have her around and no one took her flirtatious advances seriously.

As for having a drunk at the Christmas party, most of us med students were willing to volunteer, but Harry had invited his next-door neighbors and the husband, Beaker, ended up playing that role. Beaker was a chemistry professor and had been married to Mrs. Beaker for more than seven years before she became pregnant. She was eight months along and seemed a little embarrassed around a bunch of medical students. (I think she was worried that one of the happy-go-lucky students at the party would be on OB rotation when she delivered.) Beaker, after a little flirting from Tammi and a lot of liquor, became the life of the party. We were all having fun playing party games, and no one noticed that Tammi had gone into the kitchen for something to drink—except Beaker who followed her.

In the middle of a relative quiet moment in our party we heard Tammi yell out, "How dare you!" followed by a loud slap. Beaker had mistaken her enticing behavior as a come-on and tried to kiss her. Shy, pregnant Mrs. Beaker was totally embarrassed. She and her husband (with a bright red welt on the side of his face) quickly left the party.

The rest of us laughed, knowing exactly what happened and went on with the rest of the party, giving very little thought to Harry's neighbors. As a matter of fact, we really did not think of Beaker at all until the end of our second year of medical school. By then, our only clinical experiences were in psychiatry, so it did not seem unusual when the class held a special clinical-pathological conference about a psych case.

After an initial introduction by the head of the psychiatry department, Harry presented the case. He described a couple, a professor and his wife who finally got pregnant after seven years of marriage. When the baby was six months old, the mother found the napping infant dead. An autopsy classified the cause as being from what was called sudden infant death syndrome (SIDS). By this time we recognized that Harry was talking about his next-door neighbors. I am not sure it was common knowledge that the Beaker baby had died, but I guess there had been some mention of it among the class when it had happened several months earlier.

SIDS was a relatively recent diagnostic category. Although not studying about it directly, we had heard about the syndrome and we thought that was what the conference was going to be about, particularly when Harry described how the grief stricken Mrs. Beaker had gone on to have psychiatric counseling.

But then Harry went on with the case. Three months later his wife came home one afternoon and thought she heard a car running in the Beakers' garage. She went over and found Mrs. Beaker dead from carbon monoxide exposure.

The head of the psych department then took over and outlined the case, pointing out that while the Beakers had a long and seemingly stable marriage, the introduction of the baby had threatened Mrs. Beaker's relationship with her husband. The incident at our Christmas party was just an example of how Mrs. Beaker felt threatened, so she had suffocated her infant in some twisted thought process to try to preserve her marriage. She then could not live with the guilt of killing her own child and committed suicide.

I am not sure what happened to Beaker, but I know Harry was very distressed over the incident. In a way, conducting the CPC helped him address some of the guilt he and his wife had about not seeing the tragedy unfolding next door and preventing it. As for the rest of us, the message was summed up by one of my classmates leaving the CPC when he said, "Well, it might be okay to invite a drunk or a hysteric to a party, but I'm not going to invite both at the same time."

CHAPTER 11
SANGUINARY SYNCOPE

There is a phenomenon that occurs to many people, especially when they are young, that I have heard called sanguinary syncope, or fainting at the sight of blood. It is a common concern of students considering medical school. "Oh, I wouldn't do very good in medicine because the sight of blood makes me sick," they say, or, "I can't be a doctor. I faint when I see blood."

I usually tell these prospective newcomers it is no big deal. In all my interviews for medical school, no one ever asked if the sight of blood bothered me. I will say it was rather disconcerting to watch a professor pithing twenty or thirty mice for a research project while he was interviewing me for medical school. Then again, there really was not any blood involved.

But fainting at the sight of blood really can be bothersome, particularly in medical school, and I was unaware of (or chose to ignore) that possibility when contemplating my career choices. I think some of my ignorance related to me not really having seen any bloody things except an occasional abrasion on my leg when I crashed a bicycle. As I recall, it was not until the summer between my first and second year in medical school that I actually was in a hospital. By then, it was psychologically too late for me to change my mind about medical school. I had too much time and energy invested to let a little blood keep me from my MD degree.

I should have suspected trouble with blood the second semester of our first year in medical school. In one of our neurophysiology classes, we got to see our first live patient. The neurology department chairman presented a young girl in her early twenties with myasthenia gravis. She was thin and cachectic looking, kind of like a concentration camp prisoner. As we heard the case unfold, our empathy for her grew. She had started noticing some weakness in her mouth while in high school when she could not pucker up to play a clarinet. Later, she got so weak she had to be placed on a respirator and had such repeated difficulties that, even though a little stronger, she had to have a permanent tracheotomy. Recently, she had another tube placed in her throat as a feeding tube. The whole interview was fascinating to us and towards the end of the presentation I turned to my friend, Kildeer, to ask if he thought it was as interesting. Kildeer was even paler than the poor lady with myasthenia gravis. I quickly helped him lean over and he slowly recovered.

Since the rest of the year was mostly classroom work, sanguinary syncope did not strike again until the following summer when Kildeer and I got a job at a beach town hospital in the x-ray transportation department. We really did not have much to do. First thing in the morning we would bring down several patients scheduled for x-ray procedures and then take off for the rest of the day, watching various procedures and surgeries. All the attendings knew we were med students and they let us see many interesting cases. Top of the observation list were radiology procedures.

One of the first major radiology examinations we got to see was an angiogram. This was back in the days when CT scans were not available, so if a subdural hematoma was suspected, an angiogram was nearly the best way to tell if surgery was indicated. The first case Kildeer and I saw was an unconscious accident victim (unconscious until they started poking needles in him) and the neurosurgeons wanted to know if they needed to operate.

Both Kildeer and I got to see the procedure from the start. We stood on one side of the patient while the radiology resident and attending thoroughly cleaned the patient's groin and then placed a green sterile cloth with a small hole in it over the area. After numbing up the groin, they took a huge needle and stuck it through the femoral artery. This was supposed to go through the artery. They then took a stylet out and pulled the needle back until blood spurted out as high as a foot in time with the patient's pulse. At that point they knew the tip of the catheter was in the lumen of the artery and they could begin to string a guide wire, followed by a catheter, up the artery to where they wanted to study the vessels.

Before they could string the catheter very far, however, the resident looked up and asked if Kildeer and I wanted to sit down. "Oh, no," we said, neither one of us wanting to concede to the queasiness that had overcome us. "No, no, no—nothing's wrong," we said.

I looked at Kildeer, and Kildeer looked at me. Both of us were as pale as the white tiled floor that quickly rushed up to meet us. A technician helped us recover, but it took the rest of summer to regain our dignities.

There were signs that we were finally getting over sanguinary syncope by the time we were finishing the first two years of mostly classroom work and before starting the third year of mostly clinical experiences. We had a class about laboratory studies and as part of our work with blood we had to obtain specimens—from ourselves.

We were teamed up with partners to draw blood from each other. Luckily, my partner was a rather coordinated student and neither he nor I had any difficulty obtaining each other's blood. Kildeer was teamed up with one of the better athletes in our class, Sam, who had veins as big around as the test tube we had to fill. But Kildeer had a little trouble with the blood drawing technique. He applied the tourniquet to Sam's arm okay but had to poke and poke around to find a vein. Sam endured the pain gamely, knowing he would be able to return the favor. Finally, Kildeer hit the vein but was not ready for success and the needle slipped out before he could find the tube to fill. He started poking again, but Sam's arm started bleeding so badly from the first successful stick, he had to quit and move over to Sam's other arm. By the time Kildeer had successfully obtained the specimen, the rest of the class was finished and just sat around watching the spectacle.

Now it was Sam's turn. He was a little embarrassed by the whole show so instead of trying to torture Kildeer, he very quickly obtained blood. Unfortunately, it was not fast enough for Kildeer to escape an attack of sanguinary syncope. Sitting on the stool, he turned pale and only by the grace of a fellow med student who caught him, avoided falling off the three-foot high stool.

As Kildeer was recovering, Sam hovered over him. He asked why Kildeer did not even flinch while poking him multiple times and seeing his blood all over the place, but fainted when Kildeer's blood was obtained without spilling a drop?

Kildeer looked up from the floor and weakly said, "It wasn't my blood."

CHAPTER 12
MUSTACHES

In my formative years, I distinctly remember a James Bond movie in which Sean Connery, who was particularly endowed with chest hair, made the comment while being attended by a bunch of beautiful and willing women in a hot tub, that birds would not nest in a bare tree. Unfortunately, I was never blessed with the ability to grow much hair on my body except for my head, so the likelihood of me attracting girls would be as likely as swallows coming to Moss State instead of returning to San Juan Capistrano.

When I started my clinical rotations as a third-year medical student, I thought a mustache would add maturity to my countenance. It was a struggle, but luckily the first two months we spent off campus so I did not have to suffer ridicule when only patches of hair grew across my upper lip. On return, I had an acceptable bush. By now it is streaked with gray and I do not think I really need it to look mature with my white hair. Every time I think about shaving it off, though, I remind myself that it took two months to grow it before. Even if I could tolerate the harassment of my colleagues while it was coming back, I am reminded that the number of white hairs would exponentially grow. I certainly do not want to look older in the process. I also want to make it perfectly clear that the reason for keeping it is not that Mrs. Elkmoss threatens to divorce me since she only married me for the attractive growth on my lip.

I did try to grow a beard once but could not figure out what to do with the patches on the side that had no hair. I think the word "mange" frequently came to the mouths of passersby. One of these days when I get really old, perhaps when I become so demented that I cannot remember I failed at growing a beard before, I'll try to grow it again. Maybe it will work if my friends are too old or have not fixed their cataracts and cannot recognize me.

Although my first exposure to misjudging the age of a person came at my expense, I was not the one who made the mistake. As a freshman in college, my partner and I had the good fortune to be contenders for championship of the National Novice Debate Tournament. This was only open to freshmen in universities around the country and was a prestigious event. Unfortunately, I twisted my ankle the week before the tournament and had to get around on crutches. Each round of the debates was on a tight schedule and it was very difficult for me to carry two boxes of evidence cards and a brief case while hobbling on those sticks of wood. Our coach was probably even more excited than we were about our success, so he graciously offered to carry my evidence boxes to one of the rounds.

As we walked into the room, Coach naturally looked at our opponents. One of them looked more like a senior or junior in college at best, and for such an important tournament, that would be very unfair. In a big huff, he walked up to the young man and asked, "Are you really a freshman?"

The man took his glasses off and looked up. "My name is Dr. Justice. I am the judge of this round."

My partner was a lot quicker at getting to our coach (my crutches had fallen with a loud bang). "Thanks, Sir," my partner said. "I think we can make it back without your help."

We did not win the tournament but actually won that debate. The real damage, however, was that Coach would not carry my card boxes anymore. The additional load might not have weakened my ankle, but my armpits were so stressed by the crutches that they permanently stink!

Whenever I get really depressed at my inability to grow a beard, remembering I am not the youngest looking doctor in our community buoys me. That honor belongs to Dr. Goodfellow. He is an extremely competent internist, but even a mustache, which I doubt he could grow, would not sufficiently help his immature looks.

One day a very articulate retired pathologist and patient of Dr. Goodfellow's suddenly had a great deal of difficulty talking. His wife immediately took him to the hospital where a workup revealed he had had a stroke that affected his language function. The pathologist gradually improved and when I saw him back in the office several weeks later, he was actually getting his messages across rather well. I did notice him struggling every time he talked about his internist, so I helped him out by saying the name Goodfellow.

He suddenly stopped and said, "Th…thank you. Goodfellow…. I just couldn't get his name out. We always jokingly referred to him as 'Doogie Howser,' and I co…couldn't say his real name!"

So as the pressure from my family now grows to get me to shave the mustache, I keep telling them that it would make me look so young that no one would believe I was a doctor. The smirks seem to stop the conversation.

CHAPTER 13
ELEVATOR TALK

A while ago there was a story in the newspaper about a surgery resident who got decapitated trying to get through an elevator door. Makes you stop and think the next time you stick your hand in to stop the doors from closing. It underlines the dangers of elevators but that is not the only peril of what the British call "lifts."

With the increased warnings about privacy and confidentiality under new governmental rules, it is important to be careful about conversations in elevators. Take for example what happened to a surgery resident I knew, one I worked with when I was a medical student.

After psychiatry service (probably more for the benefit of my own psyche than medical education), I eagerly started the surgery rotation. The chief was inspirational to say the least. He was a typical starving resident that on morning rounds would make patients NPO (nothing by mouth) for some sort of exotic test just as the breakfast tray would arrive. He then would promptly augment his meager food ration with a piece of toast or something and continue rounds. That was not quite as bad as the previous chief who was said to have carried his own utensils in his pocket so he could filch food from cachetic patients whose lack of appetite had prompted their admission. After rounds he would take out a toothbrush from another pocket and clean his teeth before presenting to the attending.

My chief, if a little callous, was also charismatic and very helpful to young medical students, so I really enjoyed my experience with him. Near the end of the rotation as we finished lunch in the hospital cafeteria (also a place one should not discuss cases), the chief told us about an incident concerning his sister's dog. Apparently the animal had gotten sick and her veterinarian had suggested surgery. My chief promptly offered his skills and agreed to do the operation. Appropriate anesthesia was obtained (after some relevant advice of a fellow anesthesia resident), and the budding surgeon operated on the dog at his sister's apartment.

At that point in the story, the resident and I entered an elevator and joined several other people. The chief then exclaimed, "And he died! He never woke up from the anesthesia. He just died! The only thing I could think is he had some sort of liver reaction to the halothane. My sister is still not talking to me."

I thought it was funny and laughed. Unbeknownst to both of us, however, the parents of one of the patients on our service were also on the elevator. All they heard was that the resident taking care of their child had killed someone. When they got off the elevator, they grabbed their youngster and promptly signed out, not without reporting their reasons to the staff.

I rotated off the service shortly after that and never really knew what happened to my chief resident, but I do know that there was an enormous campaign by the medical school to warn students and residents against discussing cases in public places. For a short time, there was even talk about segregating medical personnel and the public from each other in the cafeteria. The CEO of the hospital did not allow such separation, pointing out that the only way he could avoid a revolt by the patients' families was to have medical students eat the same lousy food.

I recently attended a continuing medical education committee meeting and found out that the major two factors in physicians' ongoing learning is responsibility for care of a patient and conversations with their colleagues in halls, parking lots, and other unstructured places. I quickly reminded the committee that they should adamantly avoid elevators in these "curbside meetings!"

CHAPTER 14
NEUROSURGERY

When I entered medical school, I envisioned a life as a family practitioner. The first two years were concentrated in basic science and that vision changed little. At the start of the third year, however, I came under the spell of the chairman of the neurology department and I started to consider other specialties more seriously. My exposure to clinical neurology was short, just two weeks as opposed to three-month rotations in the core specialties of medicine and surgery, but I was at an impressionable stage in my medical career and it was enough to stimulate interest in neurosciences.

Our exposure to neurology during the first two years had been limited to mostly anatomy such as learning the multitude of neural pathways and memorizing cranial and peripheral nerves. That experience was fairly boring and we had almost no exposure to neurosurgery. If the chief of neurosurgery had not given us a practical lecture as second-year students, I might not really have considered it. I liked what I heard, so by the time we were setting up our fourth-year schedule and trying to decide what areas of medicine to choose for our residencies, I was undecided between family practice, neurology, and neurosurgery.

To clarify my mind as early as possible, I chose neurosurgery for my first month rotation in the fourth year. The second month I rotated on the neurology service, and then the third month I did family practice. I scheduled the last half of the fourth year at universities where I could spend a month evaluating their programs before deciding on which one to apply for a residency that would start after an internship year.

The neurosurgery rotation was one of the most exciting months for me. It was also the most grueling. I followed the chief resident, Dr. Jim, around and did all the scut work he needed such as drawing blood, writing notes, and running down lab and x-ray studies. In exchange, I got to scrub in many more surgeries. Since he was the chief, he had a better selection of cases than the other residents.

In addition to the fascinating cases neurosurgery service tended to have, Jim was one of the classiest people I had ever met. He was mild mannered, extremely handsome, brilliant, and a conscientious physician. He was married and had two young children whom he greatly adored.

Many of the young nurses also recognized what a truly classy person Jim was and they constantly made passes at him. He was on call every other night as chief resident (along with his young medical student rotating with him). One night after a particularly busy day, we were getting something to eat at the cafeteria (which he paid for). A gorgeous nurse came up to the table and, even with me sitting there, offered to join him in the call room later. Jim politely declined the blatant offer, and I was left with my tongue hanging out. When I asked him how he could resist temptations like that he explained that during his residency, particularly the chief residency year, he rarely got enough sleep. So, in addition to his wife and kids being the most important thing to him and medicine being next, sleep ranked very high. If he was ever unfaithful to those he loved, he would have a very difficult time sleeping. So he had made it a solemn commitment early on in his career that when he went to sleep, he was either going to be alone in a call room someplace or with his wife. He had never come close to violating that policy.

I learned a lot on that neurosurgery rotation with Jim, but nothing came close to what I had learned that night in the cafeteria. Another important lesson I learned was that neurosurgery was not for me. Towards the end of the rotation, Jim had arranged to operate on a patient with an acoustic tumor. He explained to me that it was a relative small benign growth that wrapped around the acoustic, vestibular, and facial nerves just as they left the base of the brain. If great care was used in resecting the tumor, the outcome for the patient was very good.

Not surprisingly, the day of the surgery was a call day for Jim. I got up at 5 a.m. to make rounds on some forty patients on the ward, drew blood work that the lab could not get, and made sure everyone was taken care of properly. The surgery started at 7 a.m. and lasted more than sixteen hours. While Jim and the attending physician peered through a microscope and meticulously dissected the tumor, I stood on one foot and another.

After the ordeal mercilessly ended at 11 p.m., we still had to make rounds on all the patients. At 1 a.m., we retired to the call room and I fell on the bed in a deep stupor. A half hour later, though, we were called to the ER because some drunk wrapped his car around a telephone pole and had a subdural hematoma.

Jim, who considered his sixteen-hour day digging out an acoustic neuroma the greatest day of his career, was enthusiastic as we scrubbed up for the operation. He must have detected a little less gusto on my part (maybe he noticed me nodding off to sleep while drying my hands) because he offered to let me drill the burr hole.

There are certain moments in medical training that stand out for me such as my first look at a cadaver or seeing my first patient dying, and this was another such moment. It was a great thrill to be actually doing something that probably was saving this patient's life, but frankly I was tired and disgusted at how this jerk could have gotten drunk and messed up my sleep. It was towards the end of the rotation and I was trying to decide whether I wanted to commit my life to neurosurgery. All I could think at the moment was, "This isn't any fun."

The next rotation was neurology. That was fun and intellectually challenging to me. Family practice rotation was much too sedate, so I decided neurology was for me.

While I never saw Jim again, I did hear about him less than ten years later. In a set of coincidences, I followed up on a patient that had been seen by a neurosurgeon in the South that I had known during my residency at Southern Fungus Medical University. I noticed Jim's name *in memoriam* on the letterhead containing information about the patient. I immediately called the referring doctor and after discussing the case with him, asked if the Jim listed on his letterhead was the same Jim I worked with when I was in medical school.

There was dead silence on the phone. Then the doctor explained it was the same fellow. Six months earlier, Jim had taken care of a young woman with a terminal brain tumor. After she died, her distraught, misguided husband came into the office and killed Dr. Jim—snuffing out the life of that truly wonderful physician.

I have never regretted my decision to go into neurology instead of neurosurgery, but I have often thought of the very valuable experience I had working with Dr. Jim and what a great tragedy to lose him in such a way.

CHAPTER 15
MEDICAL FISH

I have never been particularly fond of fish. Yes, I have gone "fishing with the boys" and enjoyed the outing, but I could have had just as much fun with the expenditure of a lot less energy watching a football game on TV. And I clearly do not have any deep desire to keep an aquarium. I view fish indoors as ranking up there with keeping plants inside. If Mother Nature intended to have plants and fish indoors, then she should have also made it rain inside. (I am told that there is one building, the huge one that houses the space shuttle, where it rains inside. As far as I know, though, they do not have fish or plants in it.)

During my medical education, however, I did have the opportunity to be exposed to some indoor fish. At first, I viewed aquariums as somewhat amusing, but soon learned that they can ruin friendships. It is difficult to think something that is supposed to provide an inner quietness—I even know of a dentist that has placed a fish tank in his waiting room to calm his distraught patients—can cause such havoc.

At the start of our fourth year in medical school, my buddy Kildeer and I planned to use his apartment with a minimum overlap, and I could check out of the med school apartments. As in most university cities, housing was at a premium, but at our "advanced" ages we did not want to share a room. It turned out that Kildeer would be away for the first two months, we would share his apartment for another two, and then my externship program would take me to other parts of the state and country for the rest of the year. What we did not foresee clearly were two problems—his fish and us being roommates for two months.

Kildeer had a giant fish tank—I think fifty gallons—and a number of fish that he carefully pointed out as he finished last minute instructions before leaving. There were a lot of small ones he referred to as guppies, and the pride and joy of his tank were two relatively large angelfish. When I asked why those two large fish did not eat the smaller ones, he explained that as long as they were well fed, they cohabitated in the tank very nicely.

Off Kildeer went for two months and things went smoothly for the first couple weeks. I dutifully fed the fish and was careful not to overfeed them as I knew that could poison the tank. Then a series of events led to the downfall of the tank. First, one of the externs on my service dropped out and that put me on call in the hospital every other night. We also had a system that the extern on call for Friday also stayed the weekend. Then too, I really had not been that faithful about feeding the fish—I might have missed a couple times. Finally, I ran out of food. I vaguely remembered on a Wednesday or so not having very much fish food, but I forgot to get more. Added to my forgetful nature was a perpetual shortage of money. When it came to a decision about a hamburger or a box of fish food, well.... Anyway, by the time my conscience made me get the food, it was the weekend and I did not get home until late Monday afternoon with a super big box of fish cuisine in hand. I guess I thought the fish would be more forgiving if they knew I had lots of food in reserve.

The two angelfish were forgiving. They actually looked bigger for the experience, but as hard as I looked, I could not find any guppies. That was okay with me, I thought. That meant fewer mouths to feed. The weekend before Kildeer returned, the planets apparently lined up with the stars in whatever sign is opposite Pisces, and I again left the fish alone for about four days. I got in late Monday night and was tired, so I still did not get around to seeing the tank, let alone feeding the fish. I use the term "fish" in the singular form because by Tuesday morning (or was it evening?), there was just one quite large angelfish left. Kildeer still assures me (when he speaks to me) that fish do not have lips, so it is impossible for them to smile. But I swear that the fish had a grin on its face from fin to fin. I know I did not have a grin and I can assure you Kildeer did not smile when he returned to see the disaster.

I tried pointing out all the best features of the new tank arrangement I could, describing how he now had a championship fish on his hands. None of my optimism made any headway. It was a very silent next two months we spent sharing his apartment with one giant angelfish.

CHAPTER 16
CALL

Even though I have made a lot of adjustments to deal with being on call, I still loathe the duty. My first experience with call was as a third-year med student, and for the first night or so, I will have to admit it was interesting. Interest quickly disappeared after getting wakened at 3 a.m. to start an IV on a terminally ill lady who had no veins left. It really was the intern's responsibility to start the IV, but most interns usually sent medical students to do their scut work if they could. First, I stumbled up to the ward and none of the IV paraphernalia (or nurse) was available. After finally finding the equipment and IV bag, I started poking the poor lady, again and again, all the time reminding myself that I was paying tuition to do this!

As an intern, my most impressive call night actually occurred the first night on duty in the emergency room. The internship started July 1st and I pulled call on the Fourth of July, the busiest night of the year. There were two new interns, a seasoned second-year resident, and supposedly a third-year resident, but he could take call at home. I do not believe I ever saw a senior resident during my internship year except at department parties. After orienting us two new interns and helping get through some of the many patients that evening, the second-year man took off for the call room at 11 p.m. He told us to give him a call if we needed help.

Things went smoothly for about an hour and then a cardiac arrest came in. This tied up both of us interns as well as well as a lot of staff, but we were handling it fairly well until another arrest came through the door. I left the first arrest and directed the second one. It was a frantic exercise, and while I was taking a turn at chest compression, a bright nurse asked if I thought we might need the help of the second-year resident. That sounded like a good idea, and I phoned the call room.

"John, we need your help! We have two full codes going and the ambulance just called and said they are bringing in car accident victims."

"Sounds like you are doing a good job," the second-year resident said sleepily. "Give me a call if I can help out."

Then he hung up. Just then the ambulance came in with the accident victims and I did not have time to call him up again. The next morning I told him I was really ticked-off. He explained that I did a good job and he knew I would be set for the rest of the year after an experience like that. In retrospect maybe it did help me be a better intern, but it was all I could do to resist strangling him with my stethoscope.

During residency, call got much better. The frequency during internship ranged from twelve hours on, twelve hours off for a two-month stretch in the ER, to as little as every third night. In residency, call ranged from every fourth to as little as every seventh night. For the last two years we could generally take call at home. Still, it was very undesirable and always limited my activities.

In private practice, call is more tolerable with better digital beepers and cell phones, but it is still a major pain. After several years of being on call every third week and then back to every other week, I was talking to my partner. He made the comment, "We should recruit a third partner so we would have less call."

That certainly got my attention, but I quickly reminded him of our experience over the years. The basic truth about call is that I hated it when I was on call every other night. I hated call when I was on every third night. I even hated call when I was on call every seventh night and could take it at home. Basically I hate call. It really does not make any difference how often I am on call—I will still hate it!

CHAPTER 17
CHARLIE'S TUNA

People in the medical profession seem to have a wide variety of hobbies. Coupled with a tendency for obsessive-compulsive behavior, this can lead to some interesting situations. Take for instance, Charlie. Charlie was a classmate in medical school and especially compulsive.

I was not really very close to Charlie, but like most of the other eighty-four classmates, I got to know him fairly well during the first two years. Early on when we were having trouble getting dates for after-test parties (some of us never did find it easy to get a date), one particularly frustrated med student observed that it would be bad news when we had our MDs and asked someone out for a date. We would not know if they really liked us or were just after our money. (That was in the days before managed care and high liability costs.) It was Charlie who pointed out, "Who cares. At least we will be able to get dates!"

During the third year, Charlie was on another tract. At the start of the fourth year, however, we shared a neurosurgery rotation together. By that time, not only had Charlie found out how to get a date, he was actually living with a nurse, Sally, in the med center apartments.

Some of the fourth year rotations were fairly laid back and easy for med students. Not neurosurgery. During that month, we generally were up by 4:30 a.m. to make lightning rounds, then back doing scut work so we could hustle on to watch a surgery case. In the afternoon we had to study to be able to brief the chief resident or attending on some neurosurgical disease or work up an admission or two. By late afternoon we were back making rounds, often until 10 or 11 p.m. If we were on call, we would be off to the ER or someplace else with a resident and often did not make it to the call room until the early hours of the morning. Then we would be back at it again at 4:30 a.m. the next morning. There were two chief residents. Charlie and I were assigned to each of them, and that meant we were on call every other day.

Neither Charlie nor I knew how rigorous the schedule was going to be when we signed up for the rotation. The first day, however, was light and that afternoon, Charlie and I got caught up on activities after not seeing each other for a while. Both of us lived in the med center apartments that were just down the hill from the hospital, but we were in different buildings. On our way back that afternoon, he invited me to his apartment, the nearer of the two buildings, for a beer and to see a fish tank that he had been working on.

I am not much of a fish enthusiast, but in the small, two-room efficiency apartment he shared with Sally, Charlie had a very impressive aquarium—actually two aquariums. One tank had something like a million gallons of water (well, maybe only twenty-five gallons, but it seemed like more) with only goldfish in it. If that was not enough, there was another tank four times as big that Charlie said was a saltwater tank. It held just two huge fish. One was a beautiful blue fish called a lionfish with long spines on it. Charlie pointed out that they were poisonous and could kill if you reached your hand in and got pricked—not a good way to die for a medical student. The other fish was a slightly larger grouper. I was impressed.

Charlie always wanted to have a saltwater tank and finally had a chance when starting his third year and moving into the apartment. There were a lot of logistical problems involved, but I could tell the project fit Charlie's obsessive personality well. The reason he had two tanks was that the saltwater fish only ate live fish and the cheapest way to feed them was with goldfish. His goldfish tank was larger than most because Charlie had to buy in "bulk" or whatever term is appropriate for goldfish in large quantities ("school" does not sound right) to get good prices. Besides, big saltwater fish need to be fed frequently and it is tough to get up in the middle of the night and run down to the local fish shop for some live fish.

The major problem in owning and operating a saltwater tank is that it must be carefully maintained and balanced as to temperature, pH, salt content, and a whole bunch of things I neither care about nor remember. But Charlie cared about them and went compulsively about getting his tank set up. He spent at least a month balancing and measuring everything and finally went to the fish store and bought his first saltwater fish. It cost him $10 (big money to starving medical students). He came back to the apartment and put the fish in the tank. Two hours later, it died.

Most people (besides not starting the project in the first place) would have just quit. Not Charlie. He got mad, rebalanced the tank, and bought another fish. This time he spent $20 since he was so confident of his skills. He did better this time. The fish lived two weeks.

This really infuriated Charlie, so he exhaustively researched saltwater tanks, rebalanced the tank, and bought the lionfish for $40. It lived and he was so happy that just the week before the neurosurgery rotation, he bought a slightly larger grouper for $20. I asked him why the bigger fish would not eat the smaller one. He pointed out that actually the lionfish would eat the grouper because he was meaner, but as long as they were well-fed ("That's why I got the goldfish, dummy!"), there would be no problem.

Towards the end of the rotation after both Charlie and I had been particularly busy and had not seen our apartments for several days, Charlie got a frantic page from Sally. Sally had forgotten to feed the fish for three days and the lionfish was trying to eat the grouper. Sally knew enough not to reach in the tank to scare off the poisonous fish, so she grabbed a broom handle and was trying to hit the lionfish to make it drop the grouper. Charlie and I were sitting at the ward desk at the time and all I could hear (along with everyone else near the desk) was Charlie's end of the conversation.

"For heaven's sake, Sally," he yelled frantically. "Don't kill my $40 lionfish to save the $20 grouper!"

I do not know what ever happened to Charlie. I do not know what kind of medicine he is practicing, or even if he is still practicing. I do not know if he married Sally, and I do not know if he still has a saltwater fish tank. I do know, however, that at our upcoming class reunion I am going to make a concerted effort to find out. Hopefully he has applied all his considerable intelligence and energies into a successful family and career.

CHAPTER 18
FLYING

One of my enduring fantasies as a boy was to fly. The costs involved, both in time and money, delayed achieving that dream, but at the end of my third year in medical school, I could see the opportunity of taking lessons. I had yet to decide on a specialty so I could imagine becoming a bush doctor in Africa and flying around to various clinics—having a time of my life. When I did start lessons, it was like a whole new dimension of the world had opened up. I started viewing my hometown in an entirely different way as I practiced flying in and out of the Moosetown Airport. It was exciting.

In spite of the flexibility in the schedule for many of my fourth-year clinical rotations, it was still a challenge to get the lessons in. About a week after I had soloed, I ran across one of my attendings while jogging around the medical school. He was a very personable endocrinologist that I had met while rotating on the medicine service. He ran with me for a little while. When I told him that I had to finish running so I could make it to a flying lesson, he brightened up. He said he had a private pilot's license but had not flown in more than twenty years. He quickly pulled out his wallet to show me the document.

I was perplexed. Here was an accomplished doctor whose schedule and lifestyle could have permitted him to fly several times a week as well as on vacations, and he did not fly. I asked him why he did not fly anymore, but he just shook his head and said, "You'll see."

I succeeded in getting my pilot's license in the fall of my fourth year of medical school but had difficulty in finding an excuse to take trips. I did make a couple hour-long flights to the South Campus of Moss State Medical University to visit some friends on the weekend, but that was about it. It was just about that time that we fourth year students were interviewing places for internships. Both Kildeer and I had not really settled on a specialty, so we were looking at general internships, mostly in family practice and someplace in the South where it would be warmer. Kildeer had gotten a Public Health scholarship, so he (along with hundreds of other scholarship recipients) was looking at one of the four hospitals where his year as an intern would be counted as part of his payback.

One day, we both received flyers about a family practice internship at a hospital less than an hour's flight from us. It had a rather well-equipped small airport, so we could fly up on a Saturday morning, look at the program, and fly back that night. What cinched the deal for Kildeer was that this would be an all-expense-paid trip including the plane rental.

On the Saturday we took off, it was a rather overcast day, but we could make the 4,500-foot elevation easily while maintaining Visual Flight Rules (VFR) status. Unfortunately, as we approached internship airport, the clouds got thicker. I was forced to fly lower and lower to maintain VFR conditions and was about at my limit of 2,500 feet as we approached the airport. The airport tower asked me to key in my transponder so he could guide us to the airport, but the old two-seat Cessna 150 did not have a transponder. The tower had our plane on its radar, though, and kept telling me the directions.

"The airport is at twelve o'clock, Cessna. Do you see it?"

I looked hard through the mist and Kildeer did the same, but we saw nothing.

"It's right in front of you! Do you see it now?" the radio screamed.

And suddenly through the mist, I could see the runway. I put the plane into a steep dive, leveled out just at the beginning of the runway, and made one of my best landings ever. Granted there were papers, sunglasses, and other paraphernalia all over the cockpit, but we were safe and sound on the ground. Kildeer looked strangely green.

We went into the airport after tying down the plane and called the family practice resident who would be showing us around. He picked us up and by the time we had gotten to the hospital, Kildeer's color had returned to almost normal. He was actually saying a few words without gulping.

We had a good day seeing the internship program. That evening we had dinner with the chief resident, the program director, and their wives. By 9 p.m. we were back at the airport for our return to Moss State University. The takeoff was uneventful and Kildeer was bubbly, talking about all we had learned about internships. We got to 4,000 feet and headed towards Moss State with the skies quite clear.

I had forgotten to tell Kildeer that Moss State University's airport was small and by 9 p.m., it closed down with only landing lights and the beacon working. That was the bad news. The good news was that at night, the beacon was very easy to see, as much as forty miles away on a clear night, and that night was cloudless (surprisingly so considering how rainy it was earlier that day).

About halfway there with Kildeer still talking about internships, I decided to increase our elevation to 5,000 feet so as to see the tower sooner. I did not notice that Kildeer suddenly became quiet. We arrived at the airport uneventfully (as well as silently), taxied over to the parking area, tied up the airplane, and drove home by 11 p.m. To me it was a great day—accomplishing something that normally would have taken up a weekend with a cost of hundreds of dollars. Not only was it free, I got in some great flying.

Kildeer, however, has never, ever flown in a small aircraft again, let alone with me. He later said that he was not too bothered by the sudden landing in a blinding rainstorm earlier that day, but he lost it coming back in total darkness when I changed elevations of the plane. For some reason or other he thought we were going to crash and his life was over.

That turned out to be the last time I ever flew a plane as well. My fourth year rotations took me away from Moss State and my internship at Beach Community Hospital left no time to fly. My residency years were certainly not conducive to flying and by the time I started private practice, I was just too far removed from piloting. I had neither the time nor the interest in renewing my pilot's license. It was then that I appreciated the comments of my old attending when he explained why he was not using his pilot's license by saying, "You'll see."

CHAPTER 19
GARDENS

Plant carrots in January and you'll never have to eat carrots. — Author Unknown

I occasionally read biographies of famous people and am impressed that many were avid gardeners. Folks like that point out the therapeutic effect of nurturing plants and occasionally refer to the benefits of eating stuff that they had homegrown. I have never quite appreciated such benefits of horticulture, particularly after my one disastrous venture.

When I started residency at Southern Fungus Medical University (SFMU), I bought a house and closed on it about six weeks before actually moving from my internship at Beach Community Hospital. After unpacking the refrigerator, couch, and bed from a rental trailer, my immediate concern was taking care of the grass which had been untouched for several weeks before the closing. I had traded a rug I had in my apartment for an old lawnmower and went about mowing for the first time. Things went reasonably well until at the very back corner, I ran into what looked like a large green log, more than two feet long. I had never seen such a plant as that. Being from the North, I thought it was just some sort of Southern flora. There were several more, so I put them in a big grocery bag and took them into the residency office the following day to show Sidney, a staff member who was also an energetic gardener.

Sidney told me they were cucumbers that had been neglected and were worthless. When I went back to the corner of the lot and looked around more carefully, I found shriveled up beans on the fence nearby and concluded that there had actually been a garden in my backyard.

I decided that the following year I would make an attempt at a garden. I frequently quizzed Sidney on what kind of vegetables I might grow and was not very excited about most of the choices until we started talking about my favorite snack food—popcorn. Popcorn plants require a minimum number of rows to cross-pollinate and I had a limited amount of space. After careful calculations, though, I thought I could pull it off.

Back home in Moss State, Mother Elkmoss helped with the project by talking to her favorite gardening store folks and supplying me with popcorn seed. To me it looked like plain old popping corn you could buy at any grocery store, but she said that it would make gourmet popcorn and I would be the envy of my colleagues.

The instructions that came with the seeds said to plant them in mid-May, which I did. I carefully nurtured them all summer. In the fall, when Sidney predicted it would be about the right time to harvest, I arranged to have a big popcorn party. I invited all the residents and their dates and planned an event that would be talked about for years to come. Perhaps it would be featured in the *Journal of the American Medical Society*. I could see it all—"SFMU resident grows the finest popcorn plants of the century!"

A week before the popcorn party, I went out to harvest my crop as it needed several days to dry out to get to just the right popping humidity. Much to my disappointment, every plant had worms.

The next day I rushed over to Sidney's office and asked him what went wrong. He asked me when I planted them and I said mid-May, just when the package from Moss State said to plant them. Sidney then pointed out that the planting season in the South starts mid-April, not mid-May. "If you delay planting," Sidney warned, "worms will get into your crop!"

It was too late to cancel my well-advertised party, so I just went to the store and bought some expensive gourmet popcorn, then put the packages into Mason jars. I popped corn for the party just like it had come from my garden. Later that evening when I thought it was safe (and people were sufficiently drunk), I made an announcement confessing that the popcorn was really store-bought and what had happened to my garden. The interns and residents said they knew my garden was a bust because Sidney had already told them. Nonetheless, they wanted to have a party and really did not care about popcorn anyway.

That was my first and last attempt at a garden. For the next two years I was there, I just mowed that corner of the yard and soon it was as if the garden never existed. Each time I came to the corner, however, I remembered with fondness my attempt at gardening. Perhaps I achieved the therapeutic benefits of gardening by just mowing the grass.

CHAPTER 20
BUZZARD

In medical school, we found out that often we learn more from our own colleagues than we do from teachers. That lesson was emphasized even more in my residency because of Buzzard, whom I met my first day as a new resident at Southern Fungus Medical University (SFMU). For some reason or another (probably because of my look of helplessness), he became a very important mentor. He was a year ahead of me and was very helpful in explaining what a first-year resident needs to know. He set me up with a couple moonlighting jobs that year, and even though he moved on to complete his third year in Texas and we only overlapped one year, we became close friends. He later was the best man at my wedding.

I was somewhat apprehensive about call at the start of my residency. We could take call at home, but still, if the emergency room (which was at a county hospital a couple blocks from the teaching hospital) called me, I was not sure I could even find the building, let alone a parking place. Buzzard, on call the day before me, offered to let me tag along with him, and I gratefully accepted his offer.

I was having dinner with Buzzard and his wife when the emergency room notified him of a consult. One of the nearby hospitals had found an unresponsive middle-aged man in their lobby with a handwritten sign pinned on him saying, "Found on the street, please help him." Since all emergencies were handled through the county hospital emergency room, they had sent him there. The ER staff of interns and residents could not see anything wrong with the patient, but in spite of poking and prodding, sticking him with needles, and even putting a cloth soaked with ammonia over his nose, they could not get him to respond. They thought he was faking, but when all their tricks failed to arouse the patient and before calling psychiatry, they consulted neurology.

On the way to the emergency room, Buzzard told me a trick he always used of producing great pain to a patient without looking so callous.

"By putting a broad key sideways between the first and second toe and squeezing," he explained, "you can really put the hurt on a patient. You can even do it while family members are standing by since they can't really see what you are doing."

When we got there, the patient was unresponsive, just like everyone had said. So with several other eager interns and residents standing around, Buzzard pulled out his key and inserted it between the patient's toes. While we were all concentrating on the foot, Buzzard squeezed. All of a sudden the man sat up and punched Buzzard in the mouth!

The next day on rounds, Buzzard explained his fat lip by telling everyone what great sacrifices he made for the new resident.

Later, in exchange for educating me about the "key trick," I told Buzzard about a procedure I had picked up in my internship year to easily extract fishing hooks. Basically, the doctor could take some fishing line or suture material and, while pushing down on the end of the hook, yank the hook in the opposite direction that the hook is in. This pops the hook out painlessly without the need of anesthetic or having to push the barb through.

The first time Buzzard tried the trick while moonlighting at an emergency room in a town about an hour away from SFMU, however, he forgot to push down on the end of the hook when yanking on the heavy suture, thus driving the hook deeper and causing extreme pain. It was said that the patient went running out of the emergency room, blood dripping, with the hook still in his arm—never to be seen again.

The reason Buzzard changed his residency had more to do with his beautiful wife as much as it did with him. Mrs. Buzzard was a gorgeous redhead, but she was also extremely shy and had migraines. Every year around Christmas time, the chairman of the department had a party, and not only invited dignitaries of the hospital and the surrounding community's prominent physicians, but also the residents and their significant others. Mrs. Buzzard, who mortally feared such occasions, told Buzzard they could not go. The chief resident pointed out that it was sort of a command performance, so Buzzard dragged his reluctant wife to the occasion. For her part, she tried to look as gaudy as the rich attendings' wives and borrowed a fake, but attractive fur coat.

During the course of the evening, Mrs. Buzzard, very much stressed, developed a severe migraine, went to the main bathroom, and promptly threw up on the floor. Now totally embarrassed, she made Buzzard take her home. After getting to their car, Mrs. Buzzard reminded him to pick up her borrowed fur coat. He rushed back, grabbing the wrong coat.

Later that evening, when the president of the university's wife reported her very expensive fur coat missing, an exhaustive search took place. When the chairman's wife called Buzzard looking for the coat, he hung up on her, maintaining he did not take the "damn" (I believe I am quoting Buzzard correctly) coat.

Exchanging coats the next morning proved to be one of the most embarrassing times of Buzzard's illustrious career. The chairman's wife was very gracious, though, and nothing more was officially said of the incident. Nonetheless, the next year when the Christmas party rolled around, Buzzard decided (or more accurately, Mrs. Buzzard told him) to go by himself.

When the chairman asked where his wife was, Buzzard made up a story that she had to attend a bowling league championship game (even though Mrs. Buzzard had never thrown a bowling ball in her life). Buzzard thought that would do, but the chairman began asking such questions as how long she had been a member of the league, her average, and what bowling alley she used. The sweat was pouring off Buzzard as the questions kept coming. The chief resident, knowing full well that Buzzard had made up the story, let him swelter.

Mercifully, the chairman was called away to his other guests, but Buzzard was a broken man. He then decided to look for another residency and by the end of his second year, moved to Texas to finish his third and last year.

I have lost contact with Buzzard for many years now, but I assume he is still in Texas practicing medicine. Only a huge state like Texas would be big enough to contain him.

CHAPTER 21
THE CHAIRMAN

Almost all the chairmen of various departments in medical school and residency I have known have been quite interesting people. As medical students, we really did not get to see many of them, but at the start of our third year I had the good fortune to rotate with the head of neurology, Dr. Brayn. It was his influence that directed me toward neurology as a specialty.

He was a short, balding, skinny man with enormous intelligence. And he was driven. Besides his career as a professor in neurology, he had outside interests ranging from long-distance running to playing first-chair cello in the city's symphony. When I first knew him as a third-year medical student, he was in his late forties and looking forward to turning fifty because it would put him in an older division in the Boston marathon where his competition would be slower.

Dr. Brayn's strongest asset was his commitment to teaching, particularly medical students. Our first exposure to clinical neurology was a two-week rotation in the outpatient setting where people often had to wait six weeks to be seen for their neurological problems. Medical students would be the first ones to interview and examine the patients. That would usually take more than an hour. We would then wait until the attending was free, then present the case. After that, the professor would interview the patient with us and direct the workup. As the orders were carried out such as getting blood tests or x-ray studies, the attending would discuss the case with us. That process would take up the morning. In the afternoon, we would see return patients, both ones that the attending was following with disorders such as epilepsy, Parkinson's disease, or multiple sclerosis, as well as the patient we had seen in the morning. During the evening we could look up all the diseases we had seen that day. It was really a great learning experience.

The second day on rotation we had Dr. Brayn as our attending. I went in to see the first new patient. It was an older lady with a somewhat overbearing husband. I introduced myself as a student doctor and wanted to go over her case if it was alright. Well, it was not alright according to the husband. He wanted Dr. Brayn and only Dr. Brayn to take care of his wife, and I could just leave.

I slinked out of the room and reported to Dr. Brayn, thinking he would just give me another patient. When Brayn heard what happened, he turned red, stormed in the patient's room with me in tow, and pointed out to the husband that his wife would see this student doctor *and* him, or she was not being seen in the clinic at all.

You would think that the following interview with the patient was a hostile one, and it was a little uncomfortable with the husband seething in the corner, but I thought I could detect a smirk on the face of the patient (which was tough to do since she had Parkinson's disease with a so-called mask-like facies).

Dr. Brayn could be extremely domineering and opinionated, but it was always consistent with his commitment to take care of patients and to educate students and residents. He was viewed as a very protective father figure of his charges, and folks either loved or hated him. There was no middle ground. I greatly appreciated the professor, enjoyed the neurology rotation, and decided to pursue neurology early in my fourth year to see if that was what I wanted to specialize in.

Dr. Brayn also got me interested in running. One of the big events he participated every year was a fifteen-mile run held near the Southern Branch of Moss State University Medical School. Since I was going to be spending six weeks that spring on a medicine rotation there, I told Dr. Brayn I wanted to run in the race. He registered me the same time he signed up.

I had been in the Army and had run several miles with everything I owned on my back, but I had never participated in formal track events and certainly had never voluntarily run more than a mile in my life, let alone fifteen. At least, I told myself, it was not a twenty-six-mile marathon.

I had six months to prepare for the event, so I daily put on my tennis shirt, pants, shoes, and socks (leftover equipment from playing tennis my freshman year in college), and started running. My plan was to gradually build up to the fifteen miles, but the best I could do was eight miles, and that was a stretch. Every once in a while I would run into Dr. Brayn in the hospital while I was on other services and he would ask me how my training was going.

"Just fine, Dr. Brayn," I would reply. "I hope you aren't worried about me beating you."

The big day finally came. It was the first long distance run I had ever seen and I got caught up in the festival atmosphere. For a moment or two, my attention was diverted away from thoughts of dying halfway through the race and having the rest of the 1,200 people in the race step on my prostrate body as they ran by. (Actually, because I was so slow and most everyone would have been ahead, I would only have to worry about a half a dozen or so people running over me.) In addition to the runners, there were thousands of supporters present. To add further excitement, the starter of the race was Jesse Owens.

I was assigned to start the race in row thirty. As I stood there, not knowing anyone else in the city, let along at the race, I spied Dr. Brayn standing in the same row. (In retrospect, since he put in my application for the race at the same time he put in his, that probably explained why we were in the same row.) He came over near the start of the race to give what I thought would be some encouraging advice. He put his arm around my shoulder and since I was about eight inches taller, I had to bend over, staring down at my worn-out tennis shoes.

He quietly said, "Elkmoss, when this is over, I'm going to take you and get some real running shoes. These will ruin your feet!"

Bang! Jesse Owens started the race, and 1,199 runners took off in unison while I stood there soaking in the words of wisdom from my mentor. I quickly recovered and started off.

At every mile, there was a table with cups of water and a counter that would sound off the number of people who had gone by. At the one-mile mark, I think my number was more than 1,000, but I kept a slow pace, worried I would not make it. At the eight-mile mark my position had steadily dropped to the mid 800s. At the twelve-mile mark, I ran into the proverbial "wall" and thought I would die. I kept up my slow pace, however, spurred on by passing many others who could not make it, until I entered the stadium for the final lap to the finish line.

Something must happen to thinking processes of runners towards the end of a long race. It is probably related to the buildup of lactic acid, lack of oxygen, or all the vital nutrients going to muscles instead of the brain, but some yahoo that I had passed walking into the stadium decided to race ahead of me. I was not going to let him beat me out of the 621st place, so I kicked it into high speed (somewhere between the speed of a snail and a turtle) and beat that sucker by a nose. I felt like Rocky Balboa after winning the world championship for the fifteenth time (or is it sixteenth?).

Dr. Brayn never did take me to get running shoes, but it did not make any difference. I never ran in another race again in my life. I got my fifteen-mile T-shirt at the end of the event and the satisfaction of beating whoever that guy was that came in 622nd.

Even though Dr. Brayn has retired, he still writes articles for neurology journals. One such essay was an obituary of the neurology chairman who had been his mentor as a resident. I wanted to cut it out and mail it to him to acknowledge how grateful

I was to have worked with him, but was afraid he might think I was offering to write his obituary. After I saw what he could do to wayward medical students, I sure do not want him to get mad at me.

CHAPTER 22
WOMEN IN MEDICINE

The number of female applications to medical schools has finally exceeded that of male applications. And while the number of male physicians still outweighs the number of female physicians, the balance is improving. If this gender equality in medicine really succeeds, I wonder if the number of male applications to nursing schools will ever exceed that of female applications?

Equality for females in medicine has always been an uphill fight. When the Johns Hopkins School of Medicine opened in 1893, it was the first school to consider female applications on par with male applications. Although it took many years, other medical schools have followed suit. I do not see the trend of nursing schools having equality in applications, however. Perhaps the influence of Florence Nightingale still prevails when she said:

Instead of wishing to see more doctors made by women joining what there are, I wish to see as few doctors, either male or female, as possible. For, mark you, the women have made no improvement—they have only tried to be "men" and they have only succeeded in being third-rate men.—Florence Nightingale

For my part, I did not appreciate the issues involved concerning equality of men and women. It was not that I paid attention to so-called "political correctness" or legislative actions such as Title IX. Most of my apathy probably resulted from my association with very accomplished females such as Mother and Sister Elkmoss while growing up, and Mrs. Elkmoss while growing "out." By the time I had started my residency, the feminist movement was well underway, but I really did not appreciate the discrimination of women in medicine.

My lack of appreciation of gender discrepancy became apparent one evening at a bar near the hospital at Southern Fungus Medical University. As a resident, my colleagues and I would stop in frequently, particularly after a day on call. One night, we were joined by a couple of CT scan techs, Sally and Mary. The CT scanner was new technology and both these girls had successfully landed their jobs over the applications of several men.

They were, of course, very competent and aggressive. Just that morning I had admitted an elderly patient through the emergency room that we thought had a subdural hematoma. At the time, our CT scan was restricted to just the head, and it took six minutes to get one of ten or so slices of the brain imaged. If the patient moved at all during the acquisition, the acquisition had to be repeated. When we tried to get a study on this ER patient, he kept moving, making Sally repeat almost every cut. After several unsuccessful attempts, Sally demanded we give the patient heavy sedation so she could finish the test.

I finally had to explain to the exasperated technician that it was more important to get a bad scan on a live patient than to have a good scan on a dead one.

That night at the bar, she and her fellow tech were explaining why they were so intense about getting great scans.

"You just don't realize how tough it is for females to get ahead in your male-dominated world," Sally said. "We have to continually prove we are better than you men."

One of the medical students rotating on the service with us tried to inject some humor into conversation. Or maybe he was just trying to be part of the group. He piped in with the observation, "Hey, all this gender equality started with giving women the right to vote. That was the biggest mistake men ever made."

The conversation changed and lighthearted comments continued. No one noticed how Sally first got quiet and then started sobbing. We finally recognized her distress. The medical student (as well as me) learned more about gender equality issues in those few moments than in all our medical school studies.

So when I read about the number of female applications to medical school finally exceeding those of males, I wonder if Sally has finally stopped crying. I am very confident that the medical student, whose name I have long since forgotten, never made another silly comment about women suffrage.

CHAPTER 23
MOONLIGHTING

I am not sure what the present policy is concerning moonlighting during residency, but in my day, most programs frowned on such activities. At Southern Fungus Medical University, my chairman took a different tact. He specifically told us not to ask him if it was okay. He said if we asked, we would not like the answer. I guess it was the forerunner some of the don't-ask-don't-tell policies adopted by the military and others.

Our chairman was a wise man in that he realized the dire financial straights most residents were in. I worked in an emergency room—a departing resident handed down the job to me. It was eighty miles away so that reduced my risk of getting caught, and for a thirty-six-hour shift from 6 a.m. Saturday until 6 p.m. Sunday, I could earn in one weekend almost as much as my month's paycheck from the residency. I was paid an hourly salary and could usually get four or five hours of sleep a weekend. I always maintained that was the most money I would ever receive for sleeping!

My biggest problem was coordinating the residency call with my moonlighting schedule. The more experienced moonlighters took the prime weekends and that left me struggling with our chief resident to make sure I was off for a particular weekend. One time when I was scouring the schedule for a spot to work, I noticed a great weekend open. Not only that, instead of the usual thirty-six hours, it was open for forty-eight hours—from 6 p.m. Friday until 6 p.m. Sunday. I greedily signed up for the weekend.

One of my greatest shortcomings during the years in medical education was ignoring current events. I missed the World Series, NBA Finals, and even Super Bowls. I had never developed interest in NASCAR races or their participants, and I certainly did not follow the racing circuit. You can imagine my shock when I floated into the emergency room Friday night to see it filled with noisy, obnoxious drunks with injuries ranging from minor cuts and bruises (from broken beer bottles) to major broken bones after falling off the roofs of their RV's in the middle of a race track. Unbeknownst to me, the little emergency room was just four miles away from one of the biggest NASCAR races on the circuit. That weekend, all sorts of injuries were herded over to my ER. I got no sleep whatsoever until about 3 p.m. Sunday when the nurses thought it would be wise to let me get a couple hours rest before driving the eighty miles back home. I think they just wanted me around to abuse again some day.

The worst moment of the weekend came during the race when it should have been the quietest. One of the more famous drivers (I guess to a NASCAR enthusiast they all are famous) had an accident. I would have said a minor accident, but at 200 miles an hour, I do not think you could say there are any minor accidents. The ambulance brought him to our emergency room with a sore shoulder. I nervously looked at the man. It was dislocated. I had reduced dislocated shoulders of patients before, but I quickly notified the orthopedist on call. The nurses asked me why I called for help, and I just busied myself with chart work.

After having more than three years experience working in emergency rooms, I swore I would stay away from them as much as possible when I finally got into private practice. But that was just a reflection of my interest in my own specialty. When I look at my experience moonlighting, I think it really improved my understanding and view of medicine that I would not have gotten in my residency alone. I am grateful for the experience and feel, perhaps, it should be made part of most residency programs.

CHAPTER 24
HOG MAW

Sometimes I hear complaints that the United States allows too many international medical graduates (IMGs) into our country. The argument, often unsaid, is that these foreigners did not grow up in America and pay the taxes that have been used to build such a great healthcare system. Some feel IMGs are taking jobs away from Americans. These shortsighted people do not appreciate that IMGs are usually the best and the brightest from other countries and contribute much more to the growth and improvement of our society and medical care than they cost. If anything, the countries they come from should be irate in that they are being deprived of the talents of many highly motivated and intelligent people.

I learned the value of foreign medical graduates early on in my residency when I met an attending, Dr. Singh. He was from India and had a very thick, but understandable accent. The very first day at the VA hospital, the outpatient department called me about an admission. It was usually very difficult to get an attending from the teaching hospital to staff admissions, but Dr. Singh was going to be there for a conference in several hours. This was going to be my first encounter with this attending, so I was particularly anxious about making a good impression.

It took me a little while to find the outpatient department, but I succeeded in locating the patient. He was a sixty-year-old gentleman without a family or anyone to help with a history. I said good morning and was greeted with, "Okay."

The patient was aphasic from a stroke to his speech center and all he could say was, "Okay." Since I had no other help than the nearly indecipherable VA chart, I labored for nearly two hours to get a history. Finally convinced that I had some semblance of information to present, I made arrangements to meet with my attending.

Dr. Singh listened intently as I explained the great difficulty I had in eliciting the history. He then walked in the room with the patient, did an exam literally in seconds, and then went out to the desk to put a brief note on the chart. As we walked away from outpatient department, I asked this obviously very astute man why he never once even said hello to the patient, let alone try to verify the history I had so laboriously obtained?

"Look, Dr. Elkmoss," Singh stopped abruptly. "After you told me that the patient was aphasic and the history was taken predominantly from the chart, talking to the patient would have been a complete waste of my time."

He went on to explain that he did not abide in residents telling him that the patient was a poor historian. To him, there were really no poor historians, just poor history takers.

The next time I presented a case to Dr. Singh, I wanted to make sure I did a thorough job. This time, the patient was in his fifties and accompanied with his wife. They were from an isolated community, not very far from the teaching hospital, but it might as well have been from a different country. These folks had never been away from the farm they worked on. His wife had noticed some personality changes, and she wanted her husband, with all his faults, back.

My first thoughts were that the patient was suffering from dementia, so I made it a point to ask him the thirty questions from a mini-mental status exam sheet I carried around in my bag for occasions just like that. The test asked somewhat simple questions such as the day, date, year, president of the United States, etc. Sure enough, my patient scored only fifteen of thirty, well into the demented range.

I proudly presented the patient to Dr. Singh and pointed out that I thought the man was demented. He listened intently and then examined the patient himself. After a couple of minutes, Singh began asking the man about his job on the farm. He asked about the man's boss as well as some of the equipment he used. My patient rattled off incredible information about farming as well as intricate details about the names of the people he worked with.

I stood in amazement as Singh examined this patient. He was obviously not demented, I had just failed to realize that my tests were based on people from my background and culture, not that of the patient's. Dr. Singh, as a foreign medical graduate, realized that naturally, but I needed to be taught.

Singh moved to start a private practice at the end of my first year in residency. Before he left, I had the opportunity to present one last patient to him. I viewed it kind of like a victory lap after racing around the neurology service for a year. I wanted it to be something special, to show that he taught me how to be a good neurologist.

Unfortunately, there was nothing spectacular about my patient's case, and I was a little disappointed until I was asking him about his family history. He mentioned that his father had died of cancer of the "maw." When I asked the patient, he just said, "You know, hog maw."

I had no idea what hog maw was, but I ran around the department and found out it was the stomach. When Dr. Singh appeared with six or seven medical students he was shepherding around for the day, I presented the case to him, briefly mentioning that the patient's father had died of "cancer of the maw." Since it did not really have anything to do with the case, and Dr. Singh did not want to belabor irrelevant information in front of medical students, he did not ask about it and moved on with the exam. Afterward, however, as we were walking alone back to the department, he asked me about cancer of the maw.

"You know, Dr. Singh," I said, winking my eye, "it's 'maw,' like in 'hog maw.' If you're going into private practice, you're going to have to know these terms!"

I do not know how Dr. Singh faired in private practice or whether he encountered prejudice because he was a foreign medical graduate, but to me he was a great example of the wonderful contributions IMGs have made to medicine in the United States.

CHAPTER 25
PINOCCHIO SYNDROME

Almost everyone is familiar with the story of Pinocchio. When he told a lie, his nose grew longer. The message was to never tell a lie, but one of my attendings, Dr. Gilbert, taught me there was more to the Pinocchio story than just warnings about deceit. Gilbert was a highly respected faculty member, and I was fortunate to rotate on his service early in my residency.

I was excited about working with him and wanted to make every moment a worthwhile experience, so when the first consult came into the department, I eagerly grabbed it. It was a twenty-one-year-old, very debilitated patient with a viral disease that was progressively deteriorating his brain. Dr. Gilbert had diagnosed the case several years earlier as subacute sclerosing panencephalitis or SSPE. On this occasion, the patient had been admitted to the pediatric unit with pneumonia. He had received adequate treatment but continued to spike temperatures. Exhaustive efforts failed to find an infection, a drug reaction, or anything to explain the fevers. At that point, they put in a neurology consult to see if the temperature fluctuations could be central in origin since this severely impaired patient obviously had all parts of his brain involved.

Dr. Gilbert was in an outside clinic that day, so I had nearly twenty-four hours to exam the patient, read all about the disease, and investigate central temperature control mechanisms. I then condensed three pages of a full consult onto the one page consult sheet, leaving enough space for the attending to write his opinion. Even with all that preparation, I was apprehensive when presenting the case to Dr. Gilbert the next day. I still could not explain the patient's temperature fluctuations.

After I had carefully and thoroughly presented the case to Dr. Gilbert, he just asked for the consult sheet, scribbled a short line on it, and handed it back. On the bottom was, "I don't know.—Dr. Gilbert."

I was dumbfounded. Here was a problem worthy of one of the medical university's greatest physicians and all he could say is, "I don't know." Dr. Gilbert apparently noted my quizzical expression. As we walked back to his office, he asked me if I had ever read the book, *Pinocchio*.

"No," I said, "but I've seen the movie."

Dr. Gilbert went on to say that like most movies made from books, the book was different. There were actually two crickets in the book, not one, and neither was named Jiminy. Pinocchio smashed the first one (the cricket acting as his conscience) early on in the book. The second one appeared later in the story. Pinocchio had stayed out all night and was delirious with a fever. The fairy godmother came to Pinocchio's rescue and asked three physicians—a crow, an owl, and a cricket—to tend to the puppet. While standing around the bed, the crow and owl offered opinions as to how a block of wood could have a fever. They finally turned and asked why the cricket did not say anything.

The insect replied, "I think that when a prudent physician does not know what to say, the wisest thing he can do is to remain silent."

One of Dr. Gilbert's pet peeves was a request for a consult that would not specify what was wanted from the consultation. It would say in the space allotted for "Reason For Consult" something like, "Neuro evaluation." I was with Dr. Gilbert one day when we received such a consult. After seeing the patient, he just wrote on sheet, "Done—Dr. Gilbert."

The ultimate short comment I ever saw happened during one of our Thursday morning neurology conferences. These were held jointly with neurosurgery, and on this particular day, the department presented a case of a patient who was demented and had signs of water on the brain without pressure effects—so-called normal pressure hydrocephalus. At the time and still to this day, it is somewhat difficult to tell which patients will respond to shunting, and the neurosurgeons wanted to know what neurology recommended. By way of introduction, the chair of the neurosurgery department, a distinguished professor himself, gave an extended description of the issues and studies concerning normal pressure hydrocephalus and then introduced Dr. Gilbert. He must have spent more than five minutes describing the expertise of my attending. After all that, he asked Dr. Gilbert what he thought about the case.

Dr. Gilbert just rose by his seat, turned to the audience, shrugged his shoulders, and sat down. The audience was stunned, but the chair of the neurosurgery department quickly recovered and pointed out that Dr. Gilbert's response just underlined how difficult it was to diagnose and treat such conditions.

Over the years, I have read countless of opinions from consultants regarding my patients, and I have noted that the longest reports are usually cases where the physician does not know what is going on. I have been tempted to borrow a small rubber stamp that generates a cricket resembling Jiminy from my young daughter and stamp it on the bottom of those excessively long reports. I do not think, however, my consultants have really read *Pinocchio* and I doubt they would understand.

CHAPTER 26
MOTORCYCLES

Doctors are often criticized for having the same harmful behaviors they admonish their patients for having. I have seen fat doctors suggesting weight loss programs and even some that smoke suggesting their chronic lung disease patients kick the nicotine habit. One of my bad habits is riding motorcycles. Yes, I know they are dangerous and are associated with some questionable life styles. After all, Mrs. Elkmoss is a nurse, and if I ever forget the long list of faults cyclists have, she will be quick to remind me.

I did not really get involved with motorcycles by plan. Luckily, I did not get involved by accident either. After medical school, I helped my classmate, Kildeer, get packed to move to his internship. He had a rusted 100cc Honda he had bought six years earlier when he was in graduate school. The first year he had driven it 3,000 miles or so, but after starting medical school (and getting a lot smarter), he just set it behind his apartment to rust. He had neither room nor interest in taking the cycle with him, so for $100, I took it off his hands. There was more than six weeks before I would start my internship and plenty of time to learn how to ride the thing.

As I went through the process of fixing it up and learning how to avoid getting smashed by cars, trucks, and assorted animals, a strange phenomenon took place—I really got a thrill from riding. Granted, the enjoyment was diminished a little when a big bug struck me in the throat going sixty miles an hour. I thought I was never going to breathe again, and respiration is especially important to a guy at high speeds on two wheels.

Despite that little problem and other assorted insects I had to wipe off my teeth, the thrill of riding a cycle was hard to get out of my system. In addition, there was a sort of camaraderie between cyclists. Even Harley riders gave little Honda owners a thumbs-up as they passed by.

I took the rusty small Honda to Beach Community Hospital where I did my internship. During that year I put more than 7,000 miles on it—more than twice than it had from the previous six years. I then moved on to my residency at Southern Fungus University Medical School where I could ride the cycle all year around. Not only that, parking was at a premium as it is at any major university, and for some quirk of fate, motorcycles could park free at the quadrangle building attached to the University Hospital. There was only one other motorcycle riding resident I had to share the big parking lot with. He, by the way, was an orthopedic resident and had a much bigger cycle. (Of course, everyone had a much bigger cycle than me.)

Even though I was in the South and rode the cycle all year around, rain could really put a damper on the joy. I had a rule that if it was not raining in the morning when going to work, I would take the bike. Otherwise, I would struggle like everyone else to get a parking place at the VA hospital, a mile or so away and the only place on campus they would let interns and residents park. Interestingly, using that rule I was only caught in the rain four times in my three-year residency.

I lived about seven miles from the hospital and the first time I got caught in the rain happened while stopped at red light about halfway home. Rain does not describe the phenomenon. Something like monsoon or "gully-washer" as they say there, might describe it better. It was relatively clear when I left the hospital, just overcast and dry, until I stopped at that light. WHOOSH! The rains instantly drenched me. The motorcycle stopped dead, and in spite of repeated jumping on the starter (it had a kick start), I could not bring it to life again. It was so rusted that the rain shorted out the electric circuits. With the traffic backed up behind me, it was worse than conducting a full code during a Fourth of July picnic.

I finally pushed the cycle off the road. Across the street was a tavern, so I dragged my drenched body into the fairly deserted establishment, called a buddy to come and pick me up, and went up to the bar to have a drink while I waited.

"Let me have a draft beer, please," I said to the lady tending the bar.

She looked up at me and laughed. "I'm sorry, sir. The wet T-shirt contest is tomorrow night!"

"Give me a damn beer!"

Once one loses confidence in a motorcycle, it is hard to get it back, so I traded it in for $150 and bought a Honda 360 (with an electric starter) for $500. Two years and 14,000 miles later, I traded that one (I got $750 for it) for a Honda CX500. I put more than 16,000 miles on it during the last year of residency.

In private practice when I first started dating the future Mrs. Elkmoss, we rode the motorcycle some. Immediately after saying our "I do's," however, she emphatically told me (referring to our co-riding days), "I did, but I don't anymore!" She has never ridden again. The motorcycle now, more than twenty-five years later, has only 18,000 miles on it.

This spring, like every spring, I got the cycle out after the long winter with the idea of selling it. I cleaned it up, changed the oil, and started it. I then drove it down the road on a nice sunshiny day and it felt great. I returned home and said, "Naw, I'll just keep it another year."

Mrs. Elkmoss thinks I am just trying to recapture my youth by keeping the motorcycle and maybe she is right. But I sure do like the feeling I get riding my Honda.

CHAPTER 27
THE VA

Back in the 1920s when the Veterans Administration created hospitals around the country to take care of the medical needs of soldiers who had sacrificed so much for their country. Many were placed near medical schools. Consequently, a lot of medical students are exposed to a VA hospital or the "VAH Spa" as it is sometimes referred.

The VA system, while created and maintained to deliver medical care, made many administrative decisions in the context of entirely different rules that often seem strange to the uninitiated. For instance, as a third year medical student, I was told to run around the ward and interview my patient before the attending arrived. I could not find many of my patients, so I was in mortal fear when Dr. Wizard showed up for rounds.

After our group introduced ourselves, he said, "Well, we better begin."

I started to stammer and stutter excuses for not being ready, but he just took off for the latrine. One medical student was a girl, so she hesitated a little before following into the bathroom. There, scattered around in a rather large area, were most of our patients. Some were sitting on the stools and others were either sitting in wheelchairs or windowsills. All, it seemed, were smoking cigarettes.

Dr. Wizard later explained that the bathroom was the only place at the VA where patients could smoke, so if you could not find your patients, then most likely they were in the latrine.

I have not been around a VA hospital for some time now, but I understand that with recent no smoking rules, medical students now just automatically go to a little brown building on the VA grounds someplace as that is the designated smoking area.

After my experience at the VAH in medical school, my next exposure was in residency. During the first year, I rotated through the neurology ward. It had about forty beds and all were filled. As a new guy, I had to make rounds and notes on all the patients every morning. That normally would be a staggering amount of work, but for VA patients, it was easy. Most of the them had chronic diseases, some quite interesting such as a patient with a rare progressive neuropathy who had been there for more than fifteen years, so the notes could be done quickly. Nonetheless, I mentally cataloged the inefficiency of the VA and looked for ways to discharge the patients to long-care facilities. Every time I mentioned discharging a patient, though, the chief resident would nix the idea.

It was often frustrating for me as a young resident to get tests done and reports back. Those inefficiencies tended to run over to the outpatient clinic as well. The chief resident came to my rescue by letting me know (in fact, insisting) that I admit five patients that day from the clinic for workups rather than taking several months to get them done as outpatients. It turned out that there were exactly five beds available on our ward that day. The way the system worked was that if you were full, the admitting office could not admit any more patients to your service. If they really had to come into the hospital, they had to be admitted by someone else (usually the medicine service) and taken care of by that service. It always seemed like we had several beds available for our own interesting cases, but no room for extras.

I survived the two months rotation on the VA service and returned to the teaching hospital for the remainder of my first year. The following year, both upcoming third-year residents had left the program and I was drafted as chief resident.

My first rotation as a much too inexperienced chief was to return to the VA. I started, coincidentally, at the same time as the VA financial year began and they had a lot of slots opened for long-care facility placement. I quickly gathered my team including a first-year neurology resident, two medicine interns rotating on the neuro service, and even a medical student. I told them to go through the ward and transfer every long-term patient that did not need any further evaluation.

These dedicated and enthusiastic folks worked diligently all week long and by Friday evening we had succeeded in transferring thirty-five patients off the ward. We were exhausted but very pleased with ourselves and met that evening at the local bar for a pizza party to celebrate our wonderful effort.

When I showed up for checkout rounds Monday morning, the glow of self-satisfaction started to dim. I was greeted by one exhausted resident who normally would have had a very quiet weekend, but since almost all the beds had been empty, he had to accept overflow admissions from services like urology, medicine, and even a few surgical cases.

While my team struggled to sort out all the admissions, I was called to the chief of neurology's office. He was a true Southern gentleman and usually very polite, but that morning he seemed to have steam rising from his scalp. For the next hour he yelled and screamed at me for ruining his service, reputation, and, I believe, even his marriage. Usually statistics are very boring to me, but he made them come alive. Prior to my clean-out operation, his service was the envy of VA. The average length of stay was just under four days, the occupation rate was nearly 100%, and the service could always accommodate important admissions.

When we discharged all those long-term patients, the average length of stay jumped to eleven months, the occupation rate fell to less than thirty percent, and everyone on the service had to take care of five or even ten new patients a day when they had previously looked forward to skating by with one, or at worst, two admissions a day!

Buzzard was a second year resident when I started and had moved to a Texas residency for his third year. He would have been chief resident instead of me if he had stayed, and shortly after my disastrous VA experience, I made it a point to call him to get some sympathy. He gave little consolation for my mishandling of the VA service. His only regret was he missed seeing the consternation on the chief's face. We chatted about his new baby and life in general, and after a couple minutes he told me he had to leave to pull duty as Medical Officer of the Day at the VA hospital there.

I said, "Say, is there any difference in the VA patients in Texas?"

"Not really," he replied. "They are basically the same. The only difference is that they wear cowboy hats!"

CHAPTER 28
EMERGENCY ROOMS

While in residency, one of the two emergency rooms I was lucky enough to work in was in a little hospital some eighty miles from Southern Fungus Medical University. It had four beds, two on either side of an open room where the nurses and doctor could have easy access to the patients. Most of the time I could get several hours sleep during the thirty-six-hour shift. It was the only job I know that I could get paid while sleeping.

By the time I was a third-year resident, I was fairly comfortable with working at the hospital and, at times, even looked forward to the duty. After all, I was familiar with the hospital, the nurses actually treated me like a real doctor instead of some sort of enemy like they did at a teaching hospital, and I was getting paid.

On one particular occasion, I call it the "day from hell," I should have known it was going to be bad. On my way to work early Saturday morning, I got pulled over by a small-town Southern cop. The road I was on was a four-lane divided state highway that unfortunately barely passed through the city limits of his town, so I guess the cop had the right to "police" it. I am pretty compulsive about setting my cruise control to less than five miles above the fifty-five-mile speed limit and knew I was not speeding. Nonetheless, there I was, sitting in scrubs in a police car, about a half hour away from the emergency room, with him tapping on his radar screen saying, "See, boy, you were going sixty-nine miles per hour. I'll be nice to you today. I'll only charge you for nine miles over. That'll be forty-five dollars."

I opened my wallet, and I had only thirty-two dollars. Seeing my predicament he said, "Here, boy, give me twenty-five. That'll leave you some gas money!"

I was going to say something, but remembered all those TV shows where the hero (victim in my case) was totally at the mercy of the small town legal system. I just shut my mouth and went on to work. Unfortunately, that turned out to be the best part of my thirty-six-hour shift.

I made it to work at 6 a.m. on time, but was still griping about being ripped off. So even if the day started out with some sore throats and other minor ailments, I had a bad attitude. Then Saturday evening came, and I was in trouble (or at least some patients were in trouble).

That night, some poor truck driver was changing a tire and it exploded. The EMS brought him to the emergency room with a hand that was dangling, completely severed except for one tendon and some skin that kept it attached. The man's scalp had been torn and pulled over his skull. The worst part of it was that he was completely awake and screaming throughout all this. After an hour and a half and a ton of pain medicine, we were finally able to get him wrapped up and shipped out to Southern Fungus Medical University. *Meanwhile, all the usual cases stacked up.*

About the time we transported the truck driver out the door, the head nurse called me into the other room to take care of an eighty-year-old lady. In the older Southern houses, fireplaces were huge, kind of like a walk-in affair. Unfortunately, this little lady stumbled in front of hers, fell in, and was severely burned. We had to stabilize her and get her off to a burn unit. *Meanwhile, all the usual cases stacked up.*

As I started trying to catch up, the ambulance brought in a man in his thirties who had been shot in the neck. He had been in a fight with his brother and a gun they were brandishing went off. The bullet had missed the trachea and carotid arteries, but lodged in his spine, leaving him paralyzed from the neck down. That required another transfer to SFMU. *Meanwhile the usual cases stacked up.*

By midnight, I finally started taking care of the usual cases. Fortunately, the nurses had triaged the cases so I saw the more serious cases first. It was past 2 a.m. when I finally got to the last case. As I grabbed the ER sheet I noticed the forty-two-year-old lady had checked in initially at 7 p.m. and her chief complaint was, "Headaches." When I approached her, she was bright-eyed and perky, sitting on the side of the examining table.

"Hello," I said feeling like I had just run a marathon, "I'm Dr. Elkmoss. It says here you are having trouble with headaches. How long have you had them?"

"About eight years," she said.

"It looks like you have been here since seven last evening. Why would you have waited all this time to see me about headaches that you've had for eight years?"

"Oh, Doctor, it was great sitting in the waiting room and watching all the action. I haven't had this much fun for years."

For the only time in my career, I told the patient to take two aspirins and call her doctor in the morning!

CHAPTER 29
DOG TRAINING

When I started my third year in residency, Southern Fungus Medical University hired a new director for the EEG Laboratory. Steve moved into a housing development near mine. A couple months after starting, he and I were talking about pets, and he told me about a Great Dane he had gotten. I always wanted a big dog, but it seemed that the bigger a dog, the more logistics problems one encountered. For instance, how do you drive around with a large animal in your car? Do you open a sunroof and have him stick his head out like the Marmaduke cartoon dog? Then too, I had already had great difficulties with my own Labrador retriever. The house I bought at the start of my residency had a four-foot cyclone fence, and the dog immediately learned how to climb it. I could imagine the fence necessary to contain a Great Dane.

Steve knew exactly what I was talking about and invited me down the street to his house that afternoon to show me what he had done to fence in his dog. When I got there, he met me in the driveway and took me around the house to the backyard. We walked through a six-foot wooden privacy fence and were greeted by a small horse of a dog by the name of Tiny. Tiny was friendly enough, but I still felt intimidated by his height. Steve then started to tell me the story of trying to contain Tiny.

There was no fence at the house when Steve moved in with his new "horse." The first day he went to work, he let Tiny stay in the three-seasons room. Unfortunately, a severe thunderstorm struck during the day. Tiny was petrified of lightning and proceeded to tear out all the screens trying to get into the house.

Repair of the three-seasons room cost the new head EEG tech quite a bit of money, plus made it imperative that he build a fence. He spent several thousand dollars putting up a four-foot fence, but the first day he left Tiny alone, the dog jumped the fence. Steve spent hours trying to find him when he got home that evening.

Several more thousands of dollars later he had the six-foot fence. I was walking over to the fence to admire the expensive arrangements when suddenly Tiny clamped on my upper arm and started dragging me away from the fence. I was terrified, but Steve quickly saved me from Tiny. He went on to explain that even the six-foot high fence was not good enough to contain Tiny, so he installed an electrified wire across the top and left for work secure in knowing the dog would never get out again.

Tiny was nowhere to be seen when Steve got home that evening. He quickly tested the electric fence, getting shocked himself, and spent several more hours trying to find Tiny. The only thing Steve could figure was that either Tiny was already over the fence when he got shocked or he was completely off the ground when he hit the wire and never got traumatized.

Steve finally solved the problem by stringing up the wire on stakes approximately three feet high and four feet from the fence. That way, Tiny was jolted before he got to the fence. It worked. After several shocks, Tiny realized he could not get any closer than four feet. Steve could eventually take down the electric fence and Tiny would stay put. I guess you could consider it a forerunner of hidden fences. Tiny also thought that no one else should get within four feet of the fence or they would be shocked, so he was just trying to protect me. Never mind that I almost wet my pants when that big oaf clamped down on my arm.

Every once in a while I think about how nice it would be to have a really large dog around, but I remember Tiny and the costs associated with just fencing him in. I just look at pictures instead. I hope Tiny led a long and prosperous life after such a rough start. He certainly got my attention.

CHAPTER 30
GILBERT THE FISH

I understand that many studies indicate aquariums have a calming effect. My dentist put one in his waiting room, but I think it leaked and ruined his blue (a color that also is supposed to be relaxing) waiting room carpet. But I really have not seen many lately. Maybe it is because, like me, having a fish tank only increases frustration, worry, and work.

My personal adventure with owning a fish tank began innocently during my residency. One of the residents was fed up with his five-gallon fish tank and wanted to give it away. I should have known better, but I offered to take it. After all, it was free.

I took it home along with the aerator and light and tried to figure out where in my little house I could put the tank. I had bought the house with a VA loan at the start of the residency. When house hunting, I looked at two houses with identical floor plans. The other house was a little cheaper but had bizarre carpeting that I knew I would have to replace before selling it. I settled for the house with new carpeting. It was one of those fluffy kinds. I did not like the green color, but I would not have to put much money into the house to sell it when I left. After all, I was not really marrying the house, just living in it for three years.

I looked all around the house for some logical place to put the tank and settled for the living room, just above the TV in a cheap bookcase I had made. Since it was the smallest fish tank you could get, it looked okay for the room.

I proceeded to set up the tank and went out to buy some fish. The lady at the pet store laughed when I told her the size of the tank and said that I would be lucky to get one fish, let alone a school that I had imagined, in the tank. It was then I spied the display of Chinese fighting fish, all in separate small tanks. The lady explained they had to keep them apart because they would eat each other or other fish if put in together. That settled it. I was going to be a proud possessor of a Chinese fighting fish.

The next problem was a name for the fish. The previous owner of the tank worked for one of the smartest professors I had ever known, Dr. Gilbert. All his colleagues called him "Gil", but we residents, of course, just called him "Sir." So that was what we called him, Gilbert the Fish or "Gill" for short.

The fish was beautiful. I was the talk of the department. I often had other residents over for some darts, croquet, or just discussions, and we would toast to Gilbert. One evening, though, someone noticed his bright colored tail fin was looking a little ragged. Sure enough, looking closer, I could tell his tail was a little off color. Over the next several days, it started looking terrible and I became worried.

My aunt and uncle came for a visit at about that time. Since my uncle was a veterinarian, I asked him what he thought. His specialty was chickens and I did not view him with the greatest respect in the world, but he immediately recognized the condition as tail rot. He explained that tail rot was a bacterial infection and that if I could get some tetracycline and put it in the tank, it should take care of the problem.

My aunt and uncle left on Monday and I got a tetracycline capsule from the hospital.

That night I dutifully opened the pink capsule, dumped it into the tank, and went to bed. Unbeknownst to me and probably to my uncle, tetracycline is a soap. Throughout the night, the gentle aerator continuously poured out pink foam that dripped down over my TV and out into the room, covering my nice green carpet. It was a disaster! It took me several days and a carpet cleaner to finally clean up the mess. The only good that came out of the experience was that Gilbert completely recovered from his tail rot.

So Gilbert remained a highlight of the residency program and I was a very proud owner until we held journal club at my house. Journal club was usually held once a month at an attending's house. Each resident would review two major articles in the literature and present them to the rest of the residents and attendings. The attending hosting the evening would provide cookies and drinks for everyone. Residents usually could not afford such a party, but the chief resident had to host the club at least once.

When my time came, the only place I could possibly get everyone squeezed in was the living room. Dr. Gilbert sat right under the fish tank. Early on in the evening, the department chair, making small talk, pointed out what a nice looking fish I had. I told him it was a Chinese fighting fish. One of the residents (someone not happy with how I made out the schedule that month) asked me what its name was.

There was a dead silence in the room until I quietly said, "I don't think I have a name for it yet. Any suggestions?"

The subject quickly changed, and thankfully we got through the evening. That turned out to be the biggest scare of my year and a half as chief resident.

Gilbert's demise came towards the end of the residency. Although I maintain I did not see a snowflake the three years I was there (that is not really true), I did experience an ice storm. Electricity went off for three days, and my house, like most, was totally electric. Not only did Gilbert's aerator not work, the temperature of his tank dropped.

On the third day of the power outage, I noticed Gilbert was listing to his side. Thinking it was the low temperatures doing my fish in, I frantically called another resident who at least had a gas stove. We put Gilbert in a baggie, rushed it over to my friend's apartment, dropped the fish into a pot, and gently heated the water. The Gill quickly righted, rose to the top of the water, gasped some air, and then died. It was a horrifying experience to us residents—almost as bad as losing a patient. We actually held a small ceremony and then flushed him down the toilet. (We tried desperately not to do that with our patients, however.)

I really could not bring myself to replace Gilbert, so I packed up the fish tank just before leaving the program and donated it to a first-year resident. I hope he experienced a much more calming effect with it than I did.

CHAPTER 31

HIGH SCHOOL CLASSMATES

My high school class was probably the largest in the history of Moose High School (MHS). Coming at the peak of baby boomers, I suffered many packed classes trying to get educated. I always felt we were extraordinary, though, but only after graduation did I realize how special we were.

There was a fairly large element of our class that liked to drag race, but since we were in the hills, it was difficult to find a flat road. In fact, the only straight one was between Moosetown and Elk Creek some twenty miles away. The dragsters, mostly my classmates, had an elaborate system including radios and walkie-talkies. When the police from one town would chase them, they could run towards the other one, their cars being faster by far. It worked nicely until about a month after I graduated from high school. The police from both towns finally got together and attacked the dragsters from both ends at the same time. The following morning, the arrest report as listed in the *Moosetown Enquirer* looked like the graduation roster.

My class distinguished itself in other ways as well. Of the more than 450 graduates, four including me, became physicians. Since I knew them very well, I can say unequivocally they were all superb folks. I consider myself fortunate to have known them, but I only saw one, Charley, after graduation. As far as I am concerned, he was the best of the best of our class.

Charley transferred to MHS as a junior and was fairly shy. Most transfers found it difficult to make friends, particularly shy people, but Charley was an exception. He was well accepted and a pleasure to work with.

I lost contact with him after graduation, but he attended undergraduate school at Moss State University like me and went on to medical school there. The next time I saw him, he was starting his fourth year as a med student orienting us new medical students. He was poised and competent. We did not get a chance to talk much, but he congratulated me on getting into medical school and told me he thought I would be very happy in medicine.

The next time I saw him was in my fourth year in medical school. I had the opportunity to do an externship at Southern Fungus Medical University (SFMU) and on my way home had stopped at a popular beach about an hour away. While walking on the boardwalk, I saw him playing a game. His wife was nearby with their two children, one and three years old. He had been in private practice in a small town in Moss State, and I thought he was taking a much-needed vacation with his family. What I did not appreciate was that he was actually going back to do another residency in radiology at SFMU starting that year.

I finished medical school that year and then a year internship at Beach Community Hospital before starting residency at SFMU. Besides the university hospital, there were a small county and two private hospitals in the complex. Nearby was a VA hospital, but the unique aspect of the complex was that there was only one emergency room. It was in a small, rundown county hospital. Since the ER served all the hospitals, the emergency room itself was practically as big as the rest of the hospital and very modern. It was also completely staffed by university interns and residents.

As a first-year resident in neurology on call, I had to assess all potential admissions to the neurology service. Even though I could take call at home, it was quite a chore when I got called from the ER about a patient. I would come in, see the patient with an intern on the service, review the x-rays and lab, and make a decision whether to admit the patient. In those days, if the patient needed a CT scan (a new device then), it would take up the rest of the night and I would end up never seeing my bed. Neurology residents actually had it very easy compared to some of the other services. Most, like surgery and medicine residents, took call in-house. Even radiology had a resident that stayed in the department all night to read studies.

About halfway through the first year and late at night, an intern and I went back to the x-ray department to review a chest x-ray. The intern had already talked to the radiology resident and told me what a nice fellow he was. This was unusual since radiology residents hated night call, especially in the ER, and usually were not very pleasant. Much to my surprise, it was Charley. After reviewing the film, I sent the intern back to take care of the patient while we got caught up with our careers.

I did not get a chance to visit with Charley after that and I deeply regret it. After finishing his radiology residency, he was visiting Moss State with his wife to check out his new practice. Late at night, three drunken teenage girls ran over the centerline and killed Charley and his wife. Not only did it tragically end the life of one of the finest young physicians I have known, it left two young children orphaned since they were staying with their grandparents while mother and father were making arrangements to move. Ironically, all three of the drunk teenagers lived.

I have missed a couple MHS class reunions over the years, but since that tragic accident, I try to make it to them just to reacquaint myself with as many classmates as possible. Mrs. Elkmoss went to high school in Swampville but seems to enjoy my reunions even more than I do—thankfully.

CHAPTER 32
ROACHES

Every once and a while, *Dear Abby* points out that it would be a big mistake for married couples to discuss their former girlfriends or boyfriends. I guess there is some wisdom in that. On the other hand, I do not think Abby goes nearly far enough with discussions of "former lives." For instance, I believe that one should not discuss prior collections of roaches with spouses. If Mrs. Elkmoss ever found out about my sordid past with those bugs, well…

Ultimately, my battle with roaches should be attributed to my medical education. It started with the medical school apartments where I stayed on and off for four years. You would think that with so many budding doctors living in a building close to the medical school that the buildings would be maintained more hygienically than they were, but I think it had something to do with the slovenly ways of the occupants as opposed to the management.

During the last year of medical school, I traveled around the country for externships and stored most of my worldly possessions in a somewhat damp locker in the basement of the apartment building. My rolled-up carpet was particularly attractive to the breed of roaches that were indigenous to Moss State. They were dark brown and about an inch or so long when fully mature.

When I packed up to move to start my internship at Beach Community Hospital, I just threw the rolled up carpet in the trunk of my car and dragged it along with everything else. It was only when I unrolled the carpet in the middle of my new apartment that I became aware of the hundreds of roaches I had imported. To my horror, they scattered everywhere. And they thrived, mixing very nicely with Beach Community's somewhat weird, long, skinny, and lighter brown variety.

A month later, after the population explosion of roaches became intolerable (I could not invite any friends over while those little insects ran rampant), I approached the apartment manager. She had received many complaints and quickly called in the exterminators. Maybe it was the infusion of the tougher Moss State variety of roaches, but the treatment failed to solve the problem. When I left the apartment the next year, the building had undergone three more unsuccessful attempts at eradicating the devils. I think they were planning on a kind of "Roach Rally" where they would invite exterminators from four surrounding districts to converge on the apartments.

At Southern Fungus Medical University (SFMU), the roach situation just got worse. Not only did I bring Moss State's and Beach Community's roaches, SFMU's town had two other varieties. One was similar to Moss State's and the other was a giant of a roach they referred to as a Palmetto bug. In the ensuing three years they also flourished, but I tended to ignore them. After a year or so, I took to wearing shoes in the house at all times, particularly in the middle of the night, so I would not accidentally squish one with my bare feet while approaching the refrigerator.

By the second year, I started a program using bug spray in various places in the kitchen and that seemed to help for a little while. When I was getting ready to sell the house at the end of my residency, though, the real estate agent, while looking over the kitchen, shrieked in terror as a particularly big Palmetto bug ran across her foot. She insisted I get professional help. At first, I thought she was referring to psychiatry, but she meant professional exterminators. I asked if that was like calling in an exorcist or something, but she did not laugh. (She was still trying to recover from her brief encounter with the entomologic world.)

I did call the exterminator, and I have to say he was impressed with not only the number, but the variety of roaches in the house. Just for the fun of it or maybe to shock me, he pulled the stove out from the wall and showed me probably a million of those creatures as well as a solid thick whitish sheet that he said represented more eggs than he had ever seen in his twenty-year career. He made arrangements to come back the next day, bringing gear similar to what I had seen in *Ghost Busters* to spray down the kitchen. He made me leave the house for four days after he set off bombs that sprayed gas in all the rooms.

I actually stayed at another resident's apartment for five days (I was feeling a little "roachy" myself and did not want to get wiped out by any residual insecticide). When I walked into the kitchen, it looked like the scene in *Gone With the Wind* in Atlanta where there was body after body laying along the railroad tracks. It took me three hours and a shovel just to clean up the kitchen from all the dead roaches, lying there on their backs with their feet up in the air. But it was worth it. My house was finally free from all those critters.

And there was another benefit from the "Great Extermination." I did not import a single roach or egg to Moss State when I moved back. Thus, for all these years I have never had to reveal my hideous past with Mrs. Elkmoss.

The guilt of living three years with four varieties of roaches still haunts me, however. I sometimes wake up in the middle of the night pressing my finger on an imaginary spray can mumbling, "Pssst, pssst, pssst….." Mrs. Elkmoss just thinks I am snoring or something.

To ease my conscience, maybe I should write *Dear Abby* an anonymous letter explaining my encounter with roaches. Perhaps I could sign it, "Roaches Without Guilt."

SECTION II
PRACTICE LIFE

The difference between God and a doctor is that God knows He's not a doctor!

Author Unknown

CHAPTER 33
STARTING PRACTICE

One of the first patients I saw in the hospital when I started private practice was Mildred. She had been admitted for an incontinence workup by a urologist. Her husband, a truly devoted man, complained about his wife's memory and he wanted a neurologist to see her.

I was fresh out of residency and eager to do a good job, but after examining the patient and chatting with her husband, I really could not see any significant difficulties. She had a perfect score on a mental status examination and her problem of bladder control seemed to be related to local mechanical causes and not any difficulty in the central or peripheral nervous system.

I remembered an old adage a professor had told us residents, "You can't improve on normal," but for some reason I believed her husband and suspected this patient had something neurologically wrong with her. My suspicions might have been fueled by the insistence of her husband or the fact that I was new to practice and wanted to do a very good job, but a new friend, Dr. Bob, a family practice physician almost my same age, says to this day I was just trying to impress the nurse who was taking care of the lady. That nurse was, by far, the most beautiful girl I had ever seen.

I had repeatedly said during my short life as a physician that I was not going to marry a nurse. I had observed many doctors who had wonderful lives married to nurses, but also saw that the divorce rate for physicians was extraordinarily high. With twisted logic, I thought that was because doctors married too close to their professions. I was reluctant when Bob suggested I ask her out, but I also made it a point to visit Mildred a couple times a day while she underwent tests. It seemed that everyone in the hospital except me knew I was enchanted with the perky nurse.

All of the tests—EEGs, CT scans, blood tests, and neuropsychometric examinations—were normal. Her bladder function was fairly well-controlled with some medicines the urologist prescribed, so we finally discharged her home with her very caring husband.

By that time, I was truly infatuated with the nurse, but when I tried to get her telephone number, she refused to give it to me. The charge nurse overheard my difficulty and slipped me a piece of paper with the number as I was leaving a patient's room. Even the head nurse was a little flustered, stepping into an empty wastebasket while leaving the room.

I called the reluctant nurse later that day, and, wonders of wonders, she agreed to go out with me. I put the date down in an office planner, so I can remember the exact date we first went out. To this day she cannot, and I am still not sure when I will let her know. I keep thinking it is an insurance policy for when I forget an important date such as her birthday or our anniversary.

I am still not sure she realizes how truly beautiful she is, but when we first started dating, she wanted to make it clear that she was reasonably intelligent. She is actually very smart (while we were dating she graduated magna cum laude from undergraduate school while working half-time and later earned master's and doctorate degrees). I thought I had some smarts myself, and I did not want to let her get the upper hand early on in our relationship.

The first time we went to dinner with her parents, the intellect of their daughter became a topic. Her mother, particularly, was very proud and wanted to make sure I knew what a wonderful girl I was dating. (My mother-in-law has since expanded her pride to all nine grandchildren, and it is truly a delight to listen to her brag about them now.)

After a little while I jokingly said, "I bet she can't spell 'ophthalmology.'"

That was like throwing a red flag in front of a raging bull. The nurse, egged on by her mother, quickly took the bet and said, "O-P-T-H-A-L-M-O-L-O-G-Y, ophthalmology," just like a grand champion of a national spelling bee.

"Nope," I said. "That's not it."

I thought I had some smarts, but that night I left any of them at home. I suddenly realized what a terrible mistake I had made. I was in a no-win situation. Either I accepted the lost bet by agreeing she was right, or risked the wrath of the girl of my dreams and her family. After unsuccessfully explaining that the word started out O-P-H-T-H instead of O-P-T-H, I asked the waitress to bring us a telephone book so we could look up the correct spelling in the physician section of the yellow pages. By that time, the whole restaurant was listening to the discussion. When I was proven correct, you could hear an audible groan from the crowd. It took weeks and a hundred dollars of flowers to finally win my way back in good graces.

Several months later, Mildred was readmitted to the hospital, and I was consulted again. This time she had deteriorated mentally and had little tiny jerks every once in a while. I repeated the EEG and it showed a pattern virtually diagnostic of a slow virus that eats away the brain called Jacob-Creutzfeldt disease. She was transferred to a nursing home and came under the care of Dr. Bob, my family practitioner friend. I had long talks with Mildred's husband (with my favorite nurse present) to explain the terrible disease and he agreed that when she died, we could get an autopsy. This was an unusual disease and potentially contagious, so I wanted to be sure of the diagnosis.

I talked to Bob as well and made sure he knew that Mildred's husband was agreeable to having this important autopsy when the time came. He assured me that he would be notified when she died so that the arrangements could be made. One of the world's leading experts of degenerating brain diseases was at Moss State University and was expecting the case.

The romance with my nurse had blossomed. Six months later, more than a year after we first met, we were married. Mother Elkmoss held the dress rehearsal dinner the night before the ceremony. She had a fetish for Cold Duck, which to me is a dark version of champagne. It is sweeter, but has a tendency to get the drinker much more inebriated than he or she realizes.

Bob was in the wedding party and was particularly smashed that evening, and was so sick the following day that he almost did not make it to the ceremony. Just before starting the service, he told me that Mildred had died the night before.

"Did you get an autopsy?" I asked.

"Gee, Herman, I was so wiped out, I forgot to remind them when they called."

Almost a year later, Mrs. Elkmoss and I were having dinner one night at a Chinese restaurant and she noticed Mildred's husband at a nearby table. We went over and introduced ourselves. He remembered us and his face lit up when he saw Mrs. Elkmoss. He introduced us to his new wife and seemed cheerful. We were happy for him. As we left the table he said, "I could tell you two were in love the first time I saw you. You are a wonderful medical family and I wish you a long happy life together."

We continue to have a long happy life together and I will always remember Mildred and her very caring husband.

CHAPTER 34
TEAM PHYSICIAN

I have long held that one of the biggest deficiencies of most residency programs is the lack of preparing folks for private practice. Most new practitioners have little idea how to establish an office, review contracts and other administrative details, let alone hire office personnel and work with hospitals. When I was in training, family practice programs came the closest to helping their graduates deal with these issues, but maybe things are better for residents starting out these days.

I griped at my department head all through my last year in residency, and when a conference came along related to starting a practice, the chairman seemed even pleased to allow me to attend. (I think he was just tired of listening to me whine all the time.)

I am not really sure I gained anything practical from the meeting about initially starting out in practice, but I viewed it as a little break in the tedium of the residency program and did learn some interesting facts that were useful later on. For example, by far and away the biggest reason that physicians practice where they do is their spouse's choice (closeness to the spouse family, etc.). Since I was single, that was hardly a bit of wisdom I could use. Years later, when trying to recruit a new partner, however, that information was extremely valuable.

Another gem of wisdom I picked up at the "Starting Out Practice" conference was that to establish myself, I should eagerly participate in community activities. So just after starting, I quickly accepted a request by a nurse at the hospital to be the team physician for a small high school football team. I have never been much of football fan (I keep up with the sport just so as not to be ostracized by "the boys"), and I certainly had no experience with sports medicine. For some strange twist in logic, though, I thought it would be in keeping with advice I had received for starting a practice. The nurse who asked me pointed out that I could actually sit in the stands since there was rarely an injury, and that appealed to me more.

What I failed to appreciate was that the nurse was using the invitation in the hopes I would ask her to come with me. I had, however, just met the future Mrs. Elkmoss (FME) and was looking for a way to prove I was some sort of macho physician.

Oblivious to what was really transpiring, I eagerly asked FME (whom I had just met on the ward) to the first big game. Later (after I asked her to marry me) she confessed that she really hated football, particularly high school, and the only reason she accepted the date was she did not have anything else to do that night.

The first home game was relatively warm, but rained continuously. It was a rather quiet ride when I took FME home, totally wet and bedraggled. Fortunately for me (or the football team as it turned out), there were no injuries.

Several weeks later, the next home game was a lot colder, but dry. FME reluctantly agreed to come. We were actually fairly comfortable, wrapped up in several blankets, when I got called to see a halfback who had developed a severe cramp in his thigh.

For the record, I maintain I clearly asked him if he got hit there or whether it was just a spontaneous "cramp" as he called it. He distinctly said it was a cramp, so I ordered a heat pack. I then marched (or did I strut?) back to my seat where FME sat shuddering in the cold.

That was the last time that FME ever accompanied me to a game. And mercifully, there was just one more game and no serious injuries (at least that I knew about). By that time, the coach refused to let me see any of his players since, if they had any fuzziness or pain, I benched them. He did not have a very good season anyway, but me taking out his better players just added to his worries. Because I had thwarted the attentions of the nurse who had asked me to be the team physician and because the coach hated my guts, I was never asked to be a team physician again. That was okay with me.

Several years later, Mrs. Elkmoss's sister married a sports trainer who worked at the hospital. During the rehearsal dinner, they asked the intendeds to share some memorable experiences. Mrs. Elkmoss's future brother-in-law quickly described a patient he saw a couple of years earlier when he was operating a Saturday morning clinic. He was seeing walk-in injuries from high school football games the night before and described a halfback that some idiot team physician had prescribed heat for a muscle contusion of the thigh.

"It was the biggest hematoma I have ever seen in all my years in sports medicine!" he said, laughing hysterically.

To Mrs. Elkmoss's credit, she said nothing about who that idiot physician might have been. I will point out, however, that if any of her kids ever get injured, she immediately calls her brother-in-law, not her physician husband.

CHAPTER 35
CONFERENCES

Since leaving residency, attending medical conferences has become an important aspect of continuing education for me in private practice. It not only gives me a chance to keep up on rapidly changing medical advances, but also allows me to make contacts in medicine—networking so to speak. Mrs. Elkmoss, however, has a different view of medical conferences. Her opinion was probably influenced by the disastrous conferences I had with my old medical school buddy, Kildeer.

When Kildeer finished his internship, he spent the next three years practicing in the back hills of Tennessee as payback to the Public Health Service for a scholarship he had obtained in medical school. I, on the other hand, went on and completed my residency at Southern Fungus Medical University and began practice back in Moss State. I kept in contact with Kildeer and visited him several times. One afternoon, while sitting on the back porch of his house overlooking the wide Tennessee River which is part of TVA's more than a million miles of waterways, I asked him what he was going to do when he got tired of the easy life in that rural setting. I was trying to encourage him to go back to a residency and join my practice in Moss State.

Kildeer looked over the idyllic scenery and just said, "Gee, I hope I never get tired of this!"

He did get tired of it after another year or so and went off to Florida to complete a residency. Meanwhile, I married Mrs. Elkmoss and settled down, expecting Kildeer to join me after he finished training. But Kildeer loved Florida and when he finished his residency, he just stayed in the Sunshine State. It was at that time that I talked Mrs. Elkmoss into letting me attend a conference in Florida. It would give me a chance to visit Kildeer while keeping up with medical education. A big bonus was that there was going to be shuttle launch the evening before the conference and Kildeer's office manager was going to take us out on his boat to watch the spectacle.

Unfortunately, the launch was postponed because of cold weather (imagine that—cold weather in Florida), so we were unable to see it. I did get to visit with Kildeer, and the following day I attended the conference. We had stayed out a little late the evening before, so during the lunch break I went back to my room and took a nap. Mrs. Elkmoss woke me up and asked if I was watching the news. I turned on the TV and every channel was showing pictures of the space shuttle *Challenger* disaster.

There were many consequences of the *Challenger* accident, but one important result was that Mrs. Elkmoss refused to let me visit with Kildeer ever again. Somehow I think she thought my trip to Florida without her jinxed the space program.

Kildeer and I outmaneuvered Mrs. Elkmoss (a very rare event) later when I finally convinced him to join my practice in Moss State. Because there were then three of us in practice, it opened the opportunity for Kildeer and I to attend what we told Mrs. Elkmoss was a very important conference back in Florida. It was a seminar on imaging that finished with a certification examination that both of us needed to take.

Our hotel was a fancy one with twenty-seven stories. Kildeer and I planned to room together (just like the old med school days) and save a little money. The first indication of trouble came when we tried to get into our room on the fourth floor and found someone else in it. We went back to the front desk and complained, noting that things already were not going well.

The lady at the front desk was very apologetic and promptly gave us a penthouse room on the twenty-seventh floor. Not only did we get a daily newspaper, but access to a room where there was a Continental breakfast and afternoon beer, wine, and snacks served every day—all for free!

That seemed quite a lucky break for us until the next morning at 6 a.m. when the fire alarm went off and some fire marshal banged on our door, making us evacuate the building. We only had time to put on some clothes and stagger down the steps (all twenty-seven stories) to stand on the street for several hours until the all-clear signal was given.

The curtains in the room with the Continental breakfast had caught on fire that morning when they were setting up the coffee machines. Not much damage was done except some smoke in the room, but, of course, the room was closed for the weekend. No more free food for Kildeer and me.

The evening before the imaging test, Kildeer and I were studying pictures, and he noticed his right eye was getting a little red. By the following day, the morning of the exam where we had to look at images flashed up on a big screen and then answer questions, Kildeer's eye was so inflamed he could not see out it. He had to wear his outdated glasses and had trouble even with his good left eye.

How Kildeer managed to take the test is still a mystery to me, but not only did he (and I, thank heaven) pass it, he scored higher than I did. (He still maintains that with one bad eye, he is a better doctor than me.)

On the other hand, Mrs. Elkmoss was not impressed with either Kildeer or her husband. She suggested that the ghost of Hippocrates was just getting even for letting us two yahoos go to a medical conference together and has stubbornly refused to let us go to anymore.

CHAPTER 36
OFFICE MANAGERS

When I was in medical school and struggling with difficult patients and their diseases, I often envisioned how to structure an ideal practice. I imagined some sort of barrier for any patient that smoked or had a blood sugar over 200, and there would be a trap door at the entry way that would shoot anyone weighing more than 200 pounds back out on the street. The office staff would all be happy, pleasant people with one mean, drill sergeant type in charge, just in case a nasty patient would slip through my screens.

When I actually started practice, however, all those visions were quickly destroyed. I gained some weight, so the trap door would have sent me out to the street, and I soon wished that I had a whole office full of mean, drill sergeant people with just one sweet, motherly type of office manager.

Just the opposite happened. I joined two other physicians on the sixth floor of an old bank building. Everyone seemed pleasant enough at the start, but I soon realized that the office manager, Mrs. Sergeant, was one tough lady. About the second week after starting, she stopped me and asked if I was taking pop cans home or possibly throwing them away. Moss State had passed a law the previous year requiring a deposit on pop cans. The office provided free soda to its workers and Sergeant wanted to make sure she got the deposit back from each can.

I told her that I might have forgotten and thrown a can or two away, but I would try to remember in the future. And I did try to remember. The next week, Sergeant stopped me again and asked if I had taken any pop cans. No, I was pretty sure I had not thrown any by mistake. That did not seem to satisfy her. When she accosted me the following week, I yelled at her and told her in no uncertain terms I was not stealing her damn pop cans.

I appealed to my partners who had known the lady for years and they just laughed. At least Sergeant did not bug me about the cans anymore. Several weeks later I heard that a couple people on the late-night janitorial staff had been caught pilfering pop cans. It was only then that I felt safe from the accusatory glare of Mrs. Sergeant. At no time in the next several years before retiring did she ever apologize.

She subsequently developed cancer, and I got a chance to see her fairly frequently towards the end when I made rounds in the hospital. She seemed appreciative of my visits, but I think she finally passed away still thinking I had stolen those pop cans!

CHAPTER 37
THE SURGEON PERSONALITY

Back in the days before anesthetics were introduced, the life of a surgeon was particularly unpleasant. It was a situation where a physician wanted to heal, or at least save the life of a patient, but to do so required invoking great pain. Even if the patient survived an operation, the resulting infection (this was also in the days before antiseptic and aseptic techniques) would most likely kill the unfortunate victim. Surgeons had to develop quite thick skins to bear up under such conditions. Even today, with all our modern surgical techniques and antibiotics, surgeons often come across as being particularly hard-core. Maybe the rigors of surgery residency have also contributed to the reputation surgeons have.

My experience with cutters, however, has been quite good over the years. I have met very few obnoxious ones, particularly in the community setting. The one exception was Dr. Blade, but he was a particularly fine surgeon. I found him to belong to a class of physicians referred to as "night fighters." Whatever the time, if I had a problem with a patient that he could help with, he was there. Not only that, he was simply brilliant. He was even a better medicine man than most internists. In addition, Blade was a strong family man and had a heart of gold. The only shortcoming was his arrogance. I do not believe I have ever met anyone more condescending than him. Patients either loved or hated him; there was no middle ground.

I first met Dr. Blade on a recruiting trip to Moss State during my last year of residency. During dinner with several other doctors in the community, he found out that I had played tennis in college. He was an avid tennis player himself, and when I returned to Moss State, he constantly asked if I would play. I really had not had a tennis racket in my hands for several years and had a lot of other things to do such as moving into a house and starting practice, so I kept putting him off.

Finally, one Sunday afternoon I agreed to play. I had seen some weather reports and it was supposed to rain, so I thought it was safe. And it was raining Sunday morning when I called him to say how sorry we could not play. He said not to worry. He had a court reserved in a new indoor facility from 3 to 5 p.m.!

I rummaged around unopened packing boxes and finally found my old tennis racket. It had a busted string, but it was the best I could do. I met Blade at the tennis court and we started warming up. I was really rusty, but if I took my time, some old strokes started coming back to me. I was a serve-and-volley type of player where Blade was what I call a junk man. He had natural swing and favored his forehand, running around backhand shots as much as possible. Much of his game involved slicing the ball.

Blade's serve was quite interesting. He had broken his shoulder several years earlier and did not have full range of motion. Consequently, he looked like a wounded bird when he served. He would throw the ball in the air, his arm would flap around, and out came a soft serve. I could hardly keep from laughing when I first saw it.

Whatever deficiencies in Blade's game were more than made up by his hustle. He scrambled around after every ball and would not give up on anything. With the combination of his energy and my rustiness, he won the first set 4-6, and you could see a little smirk on his face. The one that said, "Well I guess I showed that new guy who's in charge here."

In the second set, I had gotten over my amusement of his style and he was a little tired, so I squeaked out a 6-4 win. That really bothered him and we started the third set with intensity usually reserved for the Wimbledon Finals. The points were long and neither of us was willing to give up. It was 6-6 when we ran out of time on the court.

Two young high school girls were standing on the side waiting for their 5 p.m. starting time. Blade went over and offered them twenty dollars if we could finish the set and they agreed. After the smoke settled on the court, I had managed to beat Blade 7-5 in the playoff. He was furious, but enough of a gentleman to act fairly civil towards me. By civil I mean he shook my hand but did not say a word as he put his gear away.

Blade has continued to play tennis over the years, but I have long since put my racket to rest and taken up the game of golf. He frequently asked me to play tennis with him, but I stubbornly resisted. One day after several years, we were at a dinner recruiting another physician to our community and he asked me why I would not play tennis with him again.

I leaned over and said, "Blade, why would I ever play a game of tennis with you? I would either beat you and make you mad, or, more likely, you'd win and ruin my perfect record against you."

I cannot say if Blade's arrogance was improved by his tennis experience with me, but I can say we have been very cordial colleagues over the years. I will also point out that of all the new physicians that have graced our community, very few play tennis.

CHAPTER 38
FINANCIAL ADVICE

There is great concern over the high costs of getting an MD degree and the enormous debt new doctors bear starting out in practice. The last time I saw any figures, the average debt of graduating medical students was over $115,000. That is quite a burden, but the more I think about it, this phenomenon might have some benefits. Typically, new doctors starting private practice after years of poverty have a significant jump in their income. Many have had little education about how to manage money and end up getting taken to the cleaners in wild financial schemes by not-so-reputable financial advisors.

Take, for example, a short-tempered friend of mine in residency who was a year ahead of me. When he started practice, he bought a big fancy house, a couple of cars (twin Mercedes), a motorcycle, and even a big boat—all on credit. He seemed to be handling his financial situation (I did not notice that I paid for all the dinners we had when I was visiting him) until he got mad at his office landlord and prematurely pulled out of a five-year lease. The landlord took him to court and won $35,000. That was all it took to put my buddy into bankruptcy.

I have known many others where doctors get suckered into what are called "cow deals." They supposedly get some sort of tax credit buying calves at the beginning of the year and sell them at the end of the year at a big tax-reduced profit.

These doctors who buy into these schemes have spent their lives learning about medicine, but nothing about finances. If they had a big debt to pay off when they first started practice, then the likelihood of them mismanaging their money would be at least delayed until they could learn a little about finance strategies.

I had the example of my residency buddy fresh in my mind when I started practice. Particularly after marrying Mrs. Elkmoss and worrying about the financial demands of a family (college, weddings, etc.), I thought I would benefit from some financial planning advice. I expressed my concerns at a dinner party one night, hosted by a former president of our medical society, Dr. Know-It-All. He felt he was the most well connected person in the community and would say things like, "I know something that you don't, but I won't tell you."

Know-It-All overheard Mrs. Elkmoss and I talking about finances and he immediately told us that the only financial conference to attend was Dr. Whiz's Guaranteed Financial Success Seminar. Dr. Whiz actually was a physician and previously worked for the Food and Drug Administration. He then got into the financial seminars-for-doctors business supposedly to help guide young physicians like me as they started their careers.

True to his word, Dr. Know-It-All sent me a flyer about the next seminar, and Mrs. Elkmoss and I signed up for it. We should have suspected something when we found out it was held at a casino in recently revived Atlantic City, but we were newlyweds with no children and looked on it as just an extension of our honeymoon.

The morning lectures by Dr. Whiz were pretty good and the evenings were fantastic, but it was the optional afternoon individual counseling that proved grueling. Mrs. Elkmoss has a particular keen sense of character (except in choosing a husband), and knew at the outset that we were being hustled by offers to invest in offshore banking. We ended up skipping the rest of the afternoon sessions and had a great time. I even think we learned a little about financial planning.

One particular insight we gained from Dr. Whiz was that he detested gambling and would not waste his time at the gaming tables. It seemed a little funny considering he was gambling big-time in the stock market and tax evasive practices. He even held his seminar in a casino.

Another bit of advice we learned at the conference was to subscribe to financial journals, and I decided to receive one called *Physician Phynances*. I thought it had a cute title. I will not tell you what Mrs. Elkmoss thought of it. Imagine our shock about six months later when the monthly issue featured Dr. Whiz on the front cover. Apparently he was caught trying to get several fake driver licenses in Florida. When they tried to arrest him at the Department of Motor Vehicles, he pulled out a gun. The police shot him dead!

No one really figured out the scheme he was involved with, but it had to be a desperate gamble of some sort to warrant risking death.

Mrs. Elkmoss was only too quick to make me show Know-It-All what kind of financial advisor he had recommended. I am sure it did not change Know-It-All's opinion of himself, but I never received any more advice from him. Come to think about it, I was never invited to any of his famous parties after that either.

CHAPTER 39
THE BOARD EXAM

Of the three most traumatic experiences in a doctor's life—the first look at a cadaver, seeing the first patient die, or sitting for a certifying test—the board examinations are by far the most prolonged and in some ways the most painful. Specialty board exams usually come a couple years after finishing residency and starting practice, so they are more an individual experience. As medical students with frequent tests and two of the three parts of the National Board Examination, we were almost completely oblivious to specialty board examinations. Yes, there were subtle hints such as our attendings mentioning something about a question they were asked for their board examinations, but we students usually missed the implications until much later. I remember one professor pointing out great efforts of preparing for the exam by getting a haircut and getting his clothes pressed. When asked by a medical student what looking good had to do with the exam, he said, "I felt that if they were going to flunk me, it would be because I was stupid, not because I didn't shine my shoes."

Most neurology programs insist their residents take practice exams each year. Some even provide instruction and practice on the oral part of the exams, at least in the days when some of the examinations involved actually examining live patients like mine did. If the board exam just involved taking a written test, I do not think it would have been nearly as traumatic, even if it were a lengthy one. But the aspect of examining a live patient for a half-hour with two examiners watching every move, and then grilling me afterward for another half-hour, got more and more intimidating as the test day approached.

When I took and successfully passed the written exam six months after finishing my residency, I started to prepare for the oral portion that would be given the following year. The National Board of Psychiatry and Neurology is unique in that it provides board examinations for both neurologists and psychiatrists. The difference is that on the written board, neurologists had about three-quarters of their questions relating to neurology and only one-quarter relating to psychiatry. The opposite was true for the psychiatrists. For the oral examination, neurologists had one live and two videoed neurology patients and one live psychiatric patient. The opposite was true for the psychiatrists. So while there were some similarities between the disciplines of psychiatry and neurology, there were also significant differences.

In the period between the written and the oral exam, I married Mrs. Elkmoss. One of our first big trips together after the honeymoon was to Chicago so I could take a week-long preparation course for the boards. I had carefully selected the review course, but unfortunately, I was more interested in the location and misread the brochure. As I sat in the seminar the first day, I realized that this was a review for psychiatrists, not neurologists. When I met up with the new Mrs. Elkmoss later, she said she had figured that out already. On an elevator going to her room, she was with another wife of an attendee with a little four-year-old brat. The mother said to this four-year-old hooligan, "I love you, but I don't like what you are doing." She figured that only the wife of a psychiatrist would say something like that.

After they left the elevator, someone else said, "I don't know about you, but when I was four and started acting like that, my mother would have just whapped me on the behind. I guess you just can't do that nowadays!"

The review course turned out okay for me, however, because it was one of the few that actually gave practical experience in interviewing live patients as well as a thorough review of psychiatry—something my residency failed to do. In addition, the only day they spent on neurology was one of the best reviews I ever had. I actually felt fairly well prepared as I went off to take the board exam.

Unfortunately, there was one more major obstacle for me. The examination was given over two days in a big Midwestern city. Mrs. Elkmoss's grandparents lived in a little town about an hour away, so we could stay overnight the day before the board exam and Mrs. Elkmoss and I could visit with them. It was the first time I had seen their house. The grandparents were well into their seventies and introduced me to a card game called Skippo and a drink they called slush. Slush is made from orange juice, plenty of vodka that is frozen into an icy mixture, and served with a little 7-Up. I had never experienced it before, and, boy, did it taste great. Mrs. Elkmoss kept telling me not to drink so much, but we were playing cards and laughing. Grandma kept serving her new grandson-in-law more drink.

The following morning we had to get an early start to check in for the exam and I could hardly move. If one of my test patients had a migraine headache, I would have really sympathized with him. Mrs. Elkmoss was so mad at me for not listening to her that she made me drive.

Usually candidates are highly nervous during oral examinations and I guess I would have been too, but I was just trying to survive the hangover and Mrs. Elkmoss's anger. The first day, then, went surprisingly well. On the second day, I had recovered from the slush attack, and my first patient was a live psychiatric case, one which I handled very easily because of my review course. The last case was a video pediatric neurology case that I had no idea of the diagnosis. I struggled through the grilling that followed, but finally just told the examiners what the patient could not have and why, but that I frankly did not know what he did have. The examiners were stone faced throughout, so I thought I had flunked until, as we were leaving, one of them winked at me and whispered, "Don't worry, I had no idea what the patient had either."

I do not think there are any board exams now that have live patients to interview, but I still think the pressure and tenseness of taking such a test is still present. One thing for sure is that anytime we visit Mrs. Elkmoss's grandmother, I am always guaranteed a slush. Boy, are they good!

CHAPTER 40
ORTHO & NEURO

Orthopedics ranks right up with neurosurgery as my favorite surgical specialty. I particularly had a liking for bone doctors in my residency where the only other motorcycle rider had been an orthopedic resident.

I remember one of the first times both of us bike riders walked into the hospital. I asked him how he answered the perennial question as why an orthopedic surgeon of all people would be riding such a dangerous vehicle?

"Oh," he said, "I just say it's good for business."

My friendly association with orthopedic surgeons continued in private practice. A kindly older orthopedist, Dr. Bones, took me under his wing when I started out. He was a gruff, no nonsense kind of doctor and his patients dearly loved him. When I was getting married, it was Dr. Bones who was kind enough to throw me a bachelor's party in his substantial offices. Over the years, he had testified in so many accident cases that he knew most of the attorneys in town. He got them to stage a mock trial with a real judge and prosecuting attorney. I was brought up on charges of some sort of lewd behavior with a certain Magnolia Thunderthighs (the only Southern name he could think of).

I am not sure I can really remember much of the evening, let alone the names of my accusers. Even if I could recall the particulars of the case, I will just move along with the rest of this story. Leave it to say that I had a very good working relationship with orthopedists. That friendship was eventually challenged.

The shift in my attitude towards orthopedics began with little irritants such as when they asked me to do gait evaluations on patients with broken hips. It culminated one day when Dr. Bones consulted me to see an accident victim in the ICU with a weak leg. When I got there, the patient was in some sort of a cast and contraption up to his thigh. I told the nurse to tell Dr. Bones that when he got all those wires and stuff off the patient, I would be happy to try to evaluate the poor man. The nurse wisely never said a thing to Bones.

The loudest Bones ever yelled at me was over my patient, Ms. Hex. She was a heavy-set lady in her fifties with "spells." She was pleasant and always came with some younger ladies that she seemed to have taken under her wing. I just thought she was a kind-hearted soul, but later, when I would see some of her charges in the hospital suffering from AIDS and such diseases, I came to understand she was a madam.

The spells Ms. Hex described were weird, and I had hard time deciding if they were real seizures. After several normal EEGs and a negative cardiac workup, I decided to put an ambulatory EEG on her and see if we could capture a spell. To do that, the patient had to come to the Neurology Laboratory one morning and get hooked up to the EEG whose wires fed into a cassette box that she would wear for twenty-four hours while maintaining a log. If she had any spells, she could note the time in her log as well as press a button on the cassette box to indicate when it happened. The following day she was to return and get the wires on her head removed.

The Neurology Lab was in an old section of the hospital on the fifth floor. To get there, she had to take a small, very slow elevator that was just off the ER on the ground floor. After Ms. Hex was hooked up, she got on the elevator to go home. Dr. Bones was also coming down from the sixth floor to see a patient in the ER. While descending in the cramped, slow elevator, Mrs. Hex had a full-blown seizure. The spell was over by the time the elevator reached the first floor, but in the process, she broke her foot. Bones immediately called for a gurney and whisked the post-ictal patient over to the emergency room, X-rayed the foot, and put a cast on it before she woke up. In between all this, he paged me. When I answered, he said in a loud voice, "Elkmoss, get your rear-end down here right now and take care of YOUR damn patient!"

When I got there, he was finishing up the cast. I just smiled and said, "Thanks. At least now I know she has real seizures."

CHAPTER 41
NIGHT CALLS

The telephone on the bed stand of the master bedroom in the Elkmoss house is located on Mrs. Elkmoss's side. That seems a little strange, but on reflection, it does make sense. First of all, Mrs. Elkmoss is the real master of the house, so it is only fitting that the master, in the master bedroom, has easy access to the phone. The other reason is that I sleep so soundly that she does not trust me to answer the phone at night with any acceptable level of competence.

Mrs. Elkmoss often regales guests of the night, early in our marriage, when we did have the phone on my side. She says (and I always deny this) that in the wee hours of the morning, she woke up with the phone ringing. She then describes (and I leave the room at this point) how I was sitting up in bed holding a clock radio to my head saying, "Hello? Hello? Hello?"

Since I am out of the room at that point, I cannot defend myself. After all, I do not remember the incident. She says I just went back to sleep after saying something incoherently.

After instituting the policy of Mrs. Elkmoss answering the phone, the quality of my duties taking night calls has improved immensely.

Since she is a nurse herself, not only does she insure I am awake when answering questions, she makes sure I have given the right answer as well. After I hang up and trying to get back to sleep, I get grilled:

Mrs. E: *Who was that?*
Dr. E: *The hospital.* (Notice how I did not add—*because the folks at the hospital are the only ones that have my home number.*)
Mrs. E: *What did they want?*
Dr. E: *Some lady needed a sleeping pill.*
Mrs. E: *Why is she in the hospital?*
Dr. E: *I don't know.*
Mrs. E: *Why don't you know?*
Dr. E: *She's not my patient.*

Back in the good old days I could have withstood such a cross-examination and still gotten back to sleep. But nowadays I just lie there wide-awake while Mrs. Elkmoss, secure in the knowledge that she has contributed to medical care in our community, snoozes contentedly.

I know that in medical school as well as residency programs, physicians get extensive experience in night calls. The problem, as I see it, is that nurses have no formal education in phoning physicians at night. Only after years of talking to groggy doctors do they figure out how best to handle these situations. One veteran nurse shared with me her experiences with a physician who was known to fall asleep holding the phone in his hand. That had the added effect of being unable to call him back to wake him up. The nurse eventually sent the police to his house to get his attention.

One particular nurse is my favorite because long ago she understood that 3 a.m. was not the time to discuss a complicated medical case with a less than alert physician. When she calls me, she gives me accurate instructions as to what to order, or simply says, "Get out of bed and come and see this patient right away!"

One of the many reasons the hospital is the only place that has my home number is to make sure distressed patients get directed correctly. If they called my home in the middle of the night, they run the risk of not only getting wrong advice, but would most likely see a side of their physician they would not care to visit.

A friend of mine, Dr. Brown, told me that early on in practice he kept getting calls from a certain patient at night, always about problems that could have been handled in the light of day.

One night, Brown came home at about 2 a.m. after delivering a baby. He sat down at his desk for a moment before going to bed and saw a note from his night-calling patient that he had not taken down from the week before. Out of impulse, he just dialed the number and asked her how she was doing. She became indignant when she found out he called just to wake her up and slammed the phone down. It was, however, the last time she ever called him at night.

Mrs. Elkmoss and I were at the retirement dinner for Dr. Brown. After she finished boring the group with the questionable story about me answering a radio instead of a phone in the middle of the night, the doctor reminisced a little.

"You know," he said, "of all the night calls I have had over the years, not one of them was from a patient, insurance company, or government agency, wanting to pay a bill!"

I guess that sums it up nicely.

CHAPTER 42
SMALL CLAIMS COURT

When I first started private practice, my office manager approached me about sending an uncollected bill of a patient to small claims court. I was adamant in refusing that request. Even when we hired a collection company, I refused to sign the necessary papers to let the collectors sue my patients. I know it is a useful technique, but it just goes against my grain. It smacks of legality and since I already hate lawyers, I just do not want to do it. After all, I thought I was in a profession to help people, not sue them. My attitude might have been fortified a little by my one and only experience with a small claims court.

As an impoverished resident, I had bought a huge, but cheap, 19-inch TV set. I was very pleased with it and when I moved back to Moss State, I proudly placed it in the family room. Things went well for a couple more years until one Saturday afternoon while I was watching a football game. Suddenly, the set went blank and made a funny clicking sound. By the time I got to the TV, it returned to normal operation. I sat back down, but a little while later it did the same thing. This time it lasted more than five minutes. I finally got tired of waiting (it had already ruined the game for me), so I just turned it off and waited until Mrs. Elkmoss came home and complained to her. I turned on the set to show her, and it worked perfectly. Well, it worked fine until about ten minutes after she left for a meeting.

The next day, I carried the heavy, bulky television set to Sam's Repair Shop. It had a sign on the front saying, "You break 'em, we fix 'em." For the first time since I owned that TV, I regretted having one so big and heavy. I nearly broke my back getting it out of the car.

After explaining the problem, Sam said he would take a look at it and see if he could fix it. Several days later after not hearing from him, I called. Sam said he fixed it and I could pick it up that day.

He charged me $75, about what I paid for it in the first place. I lugged the thing home, happy I could at least watch the evening news. Ten minutes into the news, it did the same thing. So I called Sam up the next day and told him he did not fix it. He said he had, but bring it in and he would look at it again.

A week later I still did not hear anything from Sam, so I called again. He said he was still working on it. After I hung up and told Mrs. Elkmoss, she suggested I was being taken for a ride and to go get my set.

I called Sam back and told him I was going to pick it up in a half hour. He said that he had it all apart, but I said I would be taking it home in a basket if necessary and promptly drove over to the shop. It was in one piece, so it was hard to believe he had even looked at it during the week, let along taken it apart. At home I turned it on and it went, click, click, click....

It was then I decided to take Sam to small claims court to see if I could get my money back. For a nominal fee of $10 and a couple minutes filling out paperwork, I got on the docket four months later. Not knowing what to do with the TV, I placed it, with great effort, on a top shelf in our garage.

Finally the big day came for my court case. I cancelled patients for the day (probably costing me ten times what the TV cost) and lugged the TV across a large parking lot and into the courtroom.

There I sat in the back, huffing and puffing. Finally my case came up. I left the TV in the back and took my seat in front of the judge. After I told the judge my story, he asked Sam what he had to say. Sam just said he fixed the problem and that was that.

The judge then asked me if I had an affidavit or something to prove the TV was not repaired.

"No," I said, "but I had brought the TV with me and can show you."

"Bring it on up," the judge said, "and plug it in right up in front of the bench."

I lugged the heavy set up and set it on the floor, plugged it in, and turned it on. All the time I was worried that the darn TV would work, at least for the couple minutes the judge would allow for a demonstration.

Fortunately, the TV was blank and made the clicking sound. I was relieved, turned the set off just in case it decided to work properly again and stood there for his decision.

"Okay, " the judge said in a voice that he imagined Solomon would have used, "I'll award the plaintiff $75, and the defendant gets the broken TV set. How does that sound to you, Elkmoss?"

For a split second I thought that was a little unfair since Sam would be getting a TV, broken as it was, for free. But after many arguments with Mrs. Elkmoss, I had learned that if I got at least something out of a situation, keep my mouth shut. Then too, as I handed the heavy, bulky TV set to Sam, I realized that it was he who would be huffing and puffing as he lugged the set out of the courtroom.

And that was not the end of Sam's pain. Although he did send me a check for $75, years later he called the office to ask me to write a letter saying he had paid me the settlement. Seems that the court had not properly recorded the payment (or Sam had not filled out his paperwork correctly), and when he was applying for a small business loan (probably to start up another junky repair shop), the bank would not clear his letter until the case was closed.

I did send a letter, but apparently it was not enough for Sam to get his loan. He called my office later threatening to sue me for all the pain and suffering I had put him through.

My receptionist was a little protective of her doctor and asked, "What are you going to do, take Doctor to small claims court?"

It has been more than twenty years since then and I have not heard anything more about Sam or his repair shop. I pray he does not get sick and need medical care from me. If he did not pay his bill, I doubt I would violate my rule of never sending a patient to small claims court to collect.

CHAPTER 43
MEDICARE

A recent editorial in the *Swampville Daily* pointed out that Medicare spending has been growing out of control. Congress, therefore, cut payments to doctors to solve the problem. Question: Doctor bills account for less than a fifth of Medicare's costs, so how will cutting physician reimbursement control soaring medical costs?

I remember back in the sixties when Medicare was legislated. I was a young high school student and participated on the school's debate team. The national debate topic was whether Medicare should be instituted. As a debater, I had to research extensively on both sides of the argument so I could argue on the affirmative or negative side anytime.

Like all high school students (I think it is still mandatory), we had a civics class. We used to call it "Problems of Democracy" or POD, but now, at least where my kids go to school, they call it "Contemporary American Issues" or CAI. Frankly, I think POD sounds better than CAI, although neither really sings.

One day towards the end of the debate season, my POD teacher, Mr. Dilly, brought up the subject of Medicare. He was a very arrogant and opinionated man (not sweet and nice like me), and was trying to tell the class that the idea of Medicare was going to introduce communism, or at least a severe form of socialism, into our society.

Truthfully, I really did not have a clue as to whether Medicare was a good or bad idea (even now I have mixed feelings), but I did know a lot about the subject, and I certainly did not like the know-it-all attitude of Mr. Dilly. So, against my better judgment (actually I probably had no judgment at all), I got into an argument with the teacher. Since I happened to have my evidence box with me that day, I kept citing fact after fact while squabbling with him. Instead of strengthening his arguments, as the saying goes, he kept raising his voice.

Finally he yelled, "What they ought to do with old people is just give them three days food and water and send them to the hills on their own. Just like the Indians did!"

"Yeah," I said, "and look where the Indians are today." (That was before Indians began building casinos.)

That did it. Mr. Dilly snapped and threw me out of his class saying, "With your attitude, young man, you won't make it past the sophomore year in college."

Much to Mr. Dilly's (and the American Medical Society's) chagrin, Medicare legislation passed. I really did not care. I do not even think I was aware when the legislation passed, but the AMA learned a lesson about how politics works—it is not the same way we practice medicine. Since then the AMA has significantly improved their lobbying abilities (but not enough to prevent Medicare cuts).

Meanwhile, I did get past my sophomore year in college and actually graduated. After three years in the service, I returned to medical school in Moosetown. One night as a new third-year medical student on the medicine service, my team admitted Mrs. Dilly. She was an alcoholic (who would blame her since she was married to Mr. Dilly) and had cirrhosis of the liver, severe esophageal varices, and a bleeding stomach ulcer. She was not a candidate for surgery, so one of us rookie medical students was assigned to lavaging Mrs. Dilly's stomach with ice-cold saline until the bleeding stopped. I was the lucky student.

I stayed up all night with that lady, and eventually the bleeding stopped. I still had to make rounds and put in a regular day on the ward. Late in the afternoon, just before I went home to finally catch up on sleep, I stopped in Mrs. Dilly's room to see how she was doing. After all, I had a whole night's work invested in her well-being.

Mr. Dilly was there when I walked in. He looked quite a bit older than I remembered, but I recognized him immediately. I am sure he did not remember me, but as I was leaving, he said that he had heard I had done a lot for his wife and wanted to tell me how much he appreciated my help.

In my defense, one has to remember that I was very tired and worn out. As I shook his hand, I looked him straight in the eye and said, "You might not remember me, Mr. Dilly, but I'm Herman Elkmoss, the guy who you said would not make it past my sophomore year in college!"

I then turned around and left. Two days later I rotated off the service and I never saw Mr. Dilly again.

In retrospect, the AMA now feels that Medicare was probably a good idea. It certainly was not the great disaster that they had predicted. With the present projected cuts in reimbursement, however, you wonder if, in a twisted way, Mr. Dilly is having the last laugh?

CHAPTER 44
POLICING DOCTORS

Medical malpractice continues to be a very difficult issue facing medicine. Not only have the numbers of claims increased, the amounts settled per claim have skyrocketed. One of the arguments trial lawyers use to justify perpetuating the malpractice crisis is that doctors are incapable of policing themselves. Never mind that attorneys are even worse at monitoring their own actions, the fact that malpractice litigation numbers and compensation are on an exponential rise just indicates that lawyers are having more success getting doctors to testify against each other. Sounds to me like doctors are making it easier to police themselves.

Over the years as a participant on medical staff committees, I have been asked to review the conduct of various physicians. I have experienced first hand some of the difficulties in overseeing physician actions. The very first case I was involved with illustrates the issue poignantly.

Dr. Dudley was an internist in Swampville. When first starting practice, he was probably very competent but did not keep up with changes in medicine and fell behind. As his income dropped, he started ordering excessive testing and inappropriately using the hospital. One time he had admitted a healthy teenager to the hospital for chest pains, then ordered EKG's three times a day for three days to determine whether they had significant cardiac disease. All of the studies, of course, were normal. When the cardiology department complained about his competence, he always pointed out that there is no question he was a capable physician because the EKG's were all interpreted correctly. No other physician on the staff could make the same claim of accuracy!

Finally, after arduous efforts on behalf of the medical staff, Dudley's privileges were revoked. That act, though, triggered a complicated series of procedures called the fair hearing process where a suspended physician could obtain legal counsel and plead his case to a hearing panel composed of five members of the medical staff. If he failed that, he could then appeal to a hearing panel of the board of directors as well. After that, he would have no other recourse as far as the hospital staff by-laws were concerned.

As a relatively new physician, I was selected to serve on the medical staff's hearing panel with four other physicians. By this time, Dudley had exhausted the legal minds of the community defending him from the executive committee. He could not find an attorney to represent him, so he elected to defend himself. His medical practice had deteriorated so much that he had plenty of time to spend in the city library researching the issues. One of the attorneys in town reported that he saw Dudley in that library more often than any of his legal colleagues.

John Law, a hospital attorney, ran the meeting. He began by explaining that the hospital had hired him as an outside consultant to insure the hearing was conducted according to the by-laws, and he actually had no vote in the procedure. By way of introduction, he told us that six years earlier he had actually quit the practice of hospital law and moved to Colorado to invest in real estate. He lost his shirt and after five years, returned to his old law firm.

The hospital began by presenting the case in a succinct manner. Then Dudley began his defense. He rambled on and on and made little sense to the panel of doctors. After several hours, Law finally gave us a break. While Dudley was researching some additional information to bore us with, we chatted with this hospital attorney. One of the panel members asked him why he returned to practice law after quitting.

Law explained that the real estate market had taken a dive. His kids were getting to college age, so he really needed to get back earning some money.

"But I learned two important things you might appreciate," he said. "First, I believe you should take a sabbatical every five years from your practice and get completely away from medicine. It really helps prevent burnout.

"Secondly," he continued, "even though you are really frustrated with this case, you have to appreciate that the people you deal with on a day-to-day basis, like the Dudleys in this world, are really very intelligent people. Believe me when I tell you that there are a lot of dumb folks out there that you rarely see!"

Armed with that insight, we returned to the hearing and struggled through the marathon. In the end, we upheld the suspension of privileges. The hospital board also denied Dudley his appeal and I thought that was the end of the matter. Unfortunately, Dudley was very thorough in his legal research and filed a $100 million lawsuit against the hospital. In the suit, several physicians were named including three of the five of us who were involved in his fair hearing procedure. For some twisted reason, I was not included.

The case was eventually dismissed, but the angst of the physicians involved, despite being constantly consoled by hospital attorneys (whom we have grown to mistrust), was considerable. I was celebrating with one of the physicians named in the suit just after we received the good news. He reiterated that these types of things just make it even more difficult to police ourselves. I agreed, but I pointed out that the worst consequence of the suit being dropped was that his value had just decreased by $100 million!

CHAPTER 45
ATTORNEYS

The animosity between medical and legal professions is probably well deserved, but I am getting a little more tolerant these days. I am not saying lawyers do not tick me off considerably, but lately I am getting a little less irritated. I have come to realize, like a friend of mine says, "Ninety-eight percent of the attorneys give the other two percent a bad name." In all my dealings with lawyers, though, I really can remember only one halfway satisfactory outcome. It had to do with a patient named Beverly.

I first met Beverly as an indigent single female with two young children. She had been admitted to the hospital after suffering several convulsions in a row. Her seizures were brought under control fairly easily with medicine, but she was quite slow mentally, and it was difficult to maintain her in therapeutic range because of compliance. Beverly was hospitalized every other month or so with breakthrough seizures and found to have low blood levels of anticonvulsants. Each time, social service not only would have to provide outpatient assistance to insure she got her medicine, but help make sure her children were adequately taken care of.

After a couple of years of this, the child protective agency became involved and took steps to remove Beverly's kids from her care. It was then that I heard from Attorney Dimwit for the first time. He had been assigned to represent her interest in the child custody case and wrote to me to get a copy of her records. When our office sent him back a standard letter requesting a proper release of records from the patient and $25 to cover the costs, Beverly's attorney became irate.

"I am taking this case *pro bono*, so I'm sure you don't want me to tell the judge that you are obstructing justice by charging me a fee for a copy of my client's records," Dimwit wrote back (probably costing his secretary and him much more than $25 worth of time and effort).

I looked carefully at Dimwit's letter. The judge he referred to was the same one who presided over my bachelor's party several years earlier. I quickly wrote back (with a copy to the judge) that when he discussed the matter with the court, point out that I had taken care of this indigent patient for several years and provided thousands of dollars of non-reimbursed care for her. That paled when compared to the more than $100,000 the hospital had provided. I concluded by saying, "And to think you are concerned with a $25 charge for her records! Nonetheless, I'll split the difference. If you send a check for $12.50 and an apology, I'd be happy to send along a copy of her extensive records."

Shortly after that I received a handwritten note asking me to "forgive a crotchety old lawyer" and a check for $12.50. We sent him back a copy of Beverly's records, the un-cashed check, and a note saying we really were not as interested in his or her money as much as we were in her welfare. We hoped she was being well represented.

Several years later, I was asked to see Dimwit as a patient when he suffered a short, mild seizure. His brain scan showed multiple tumors in his brain and further investigation revealed that he had lung cancer that had spread. After the oncologist had seen him and discussed all his treatment options, he had decided not to go through any further therapy. I visited him one last time and found him in the visitors' lounge instead of his room. It was the only place in the hospital at the time that permitted smoking.

He was standing in the middle of the room with a cigarette in his hand explaining his decision not to have radiation therapy. The ash got longer and longer as we stood there talking, and I was getting concerned it would fall on the floor. He asked me if I thought he had gotten cancer from scuba diving off the Pacific Coast the previous year.

"You don't think it had anything to do with that?" I said, pointing to the cigarette he was holding in his hand.

"Oh," he replied, "you doctors have never proved that smoking causes cancer."

That was the last time I saw Attorney Dimwit, standing there holding a cigarette in his hand with a ridiculously long ash. He died shortly after that. Twenty-some years later, I am still seeing Beverly as a patient. She continues to have a little difficulty getting her medicines and has an occasional breakthrough seizure, but she is getting along fairly nicely because of a lot of help from many people.

I have often thought about why there is so much animosity between doctors and lawyers. At least one of the factors seems to be that medicine considers life priceless and attorneys often have to put dollar signs to "life, liberty, and the pursuit of happiness." In Beverly's case, it appears that life has won out.

CHAPTER 46
HANDWRITING

There is an old story about a rich lady who was going to give a dinner party for prominent people in town. She could not read the RSVP from her doctor because his handwriting was so lousy.

"Here," she said to her servant, "take this down to the pharmacist. He's used to doctors' handwriting. Ask him what it says."

After a little while the servant returned and the lady asked, "Well, is the doctor coming or not?"

The servant shrugged his shoulders and said, "I don't know. The pharmacist just gave me this bottle of pills and charged me $20!"

The Institute of Medicine suggested at one point that there are up to 98,000 unnecessary deaths a year in U.S. hospitals as a result of medical errors. A big proportion of those errors were related to bad physician handwriting and the problem of poor legibility, again, came to the forefront.

From a personal standpoint, I have suffered terribly from my own bad handwriting. I cannot tell you how many telephone calls

I get from the floor just after I leave (or occasionally several hours after I have written STAT orders) because the ward clerk or nurse cannot read my writing. It is bad enough to risk wrong orders for the patient, but poor handwriting has cost thousands of hours of lost time to me and the already overworked nurses and hospital staff, trying to read them. One exasperated nurse finally asked me if I had taken the doctors' handwriting class twice in medical school. "You know," she said, "the one just after the golf seminar?"

Mrs. Elkmoss, a nurse herself, has even formed a support group. As an occasional visitor to the hospital to teach nursing students, she, along with fellow nurses, formed an elaborate network to locate her when I have visited the floor so that she can interpret my scratches. I knew I was in trouble when she came up to me, glowing from the strain of trying to read my scrawl (Mrs. Elkmoss does not sweat or perspire—she glows), and asked me to read it for her. I could not, but to cover up an embarrassing moment, I reissued a completely new set of orders. After all, no one could argue that it was not what I originally wrote.

Which leads to the real purpose of this essay. What can be done about bad handwriting? I have struggled with this issue for many years. Like most people with bad habits they recognize, I felt I could handle the problem myself. "If I would just slow down," I said to myself, "my handwriting will be okay." I dutifully put "Improve Handwriting" on my New Year's resolutions, but in the recent decade, it has only taken one trip on rounds to forget it.

Finally understanding that New Year's resolutions do nothing except generate a brief (very brief) reprieve from nagging spouses (even though Mrs. Elkmoss does not frequent the hospital as much anymore, she still gets calls from desperate nurses), I opted to develop interest in a writing seminar. One day, I was on the telephone trying to talk a course director into including a class on handwriting. My partner, Kildeer, three offices away, fell off his chair laughing. Still guffawing and rubbing a sore elbow from his fall, he commented, "You giving a talk about bad handwriting is like Hitler talking about world peace!"

Needless to say, I gave up that approach. When Personal Digital Assistants (PDA's) came out, I was encouraged to think many of my problems might be solved. After all, I understood I would be able to e-mail prescriptions to the pharmacy (even RSVP's?). I could submit my billing quicker and more accurately, and when the hospital went on-line, I could write all my orders that way. I even took a course in PDA's, but when it came to graffiti writing, my palm pilot almost blew up. The panicked seminar leader rushed over, took the palm pilot out of my hands, and told me to stick to typing! Not being a fan of lugging a typewriter pad around with me all day, I have temporarily put use of PDA's off my list of "to do" things.

The solution to my handwriting problem finally came in an editorial by Dr. Charles Davant in the *Medical Economics* magazine. He also suffered from bad handwriting. His is actually worse than mine (trust me, I've seen it), and his hospital got in big trouble with Medicare because they could not read his signature on discharge records. Medicare has a rule: If it can't be read, it does not exist.

When Davant's hospital got severely dinged by the reviewers because of his handwriting, he cleverly got a psychology friend of his to verify that he was "handwriting impaired." The hospital informed Medicare that Dr. Davant had a learning disability and was going to sue them and the reviewers for harassing and discriminating against a "differently abled" American. It worked, and the reviewers backed off!

So there is the solution to my problem. I can try to get a psychologist to declare me impaired and then I can apply under some sort of government program for an electric cart with a typing pad and PDA (maybe I could get a remote one like I have seen for golfers that just follow them around the course with their clubs, stopping when they do). Then, I would never hand-write a note again. Alas, it would be my luck that the psychologist I picked would agree that I was impaired all right, but psychologically, and try to lock me up.

CHAPTER 47
NURSING SHORTAGE

We are faced with a serious nursing shortage. It is a complex issue and as a caring physician, I did what any other reasonable person would do to understand it—I went surfing on the net. After a couple of hours and a migraine headache, I realized that the issue was much too complicated for me to comprehend. I did glean some information, though. Let me share excerpts from the first three responses nurses had to a recent online article about the nursing shortage. The first said, "I believe the problem in nursing today is that nurses receive very little respect…" The next one was, "One of these problems is that we continue to be devalued by not only physicians and administrators, but by the general public as well." And the next was, "Reason Number One: Nurses are not respected."

Now I am not that naive to think lack of respect is the only reason for our nursing shortage, but it certainly seems to be a major contributor. I learned early in my career that physicians need to treat nurses as the colleagues they are. The trouble is that I continually need to be reminded.

Beach Community Hospital, where I spent my internship year, was a 650-bed hospital that also had an annex used as a rehab unit. One of our duties as interns on call was to insert all NG tubes in the hospital as well as the annex.

Early in the year and late at night, the rehab unit called me. The nurse was pleasant and asked if I could come over and put in an NG tube. I was tired and asked if it was really an emergency. She said it was for a diabetic that had just gotten insulin and needed her feedings or she would go into insulin shock.

I dragged myself over and found a tragic fourteen-year-old girl who had been involved in a car accident a month or so earlier. The right side of her head was severely damaged and she was paralyzed on the left side. While not totally comatose, the little girl could not follow commands and was quite agitated, constantly pulling on things such as the NG tube with her right hand. In spite of restraints (those were the days when we did not have to write copious notes to justify restraining patients), she managed to worm out of her shackles and got the NG tube out.

I reinserted the tube and returned to the call room for a few minutes rest until I got called to admit a patient out of the emergency room. I did not give the incident much thought until the next week when I was on call again. This time the nurse on duty called a little earlier in the evening and I quickly took care of the reinsertion. When I got awakened in the middle of the night the next time I was on call, I became irritated.

"Can't I just start it later when I have to get up for an admission or something?"

"No, Doctor. She just had insulin and she needs her feedings."

"Why can't you put it in? You've seen me do it plenty of times."

"No, Doctor. It's against the rules."

So at 3 a.m., I stumbled to the rehab unit. By this time I already knew where she was and went directly the patient's room. There was no NG tube or lubricant, so I went out to the desk and yelled at the nurse.

"Where's the da-blamed NG tube? Do I have to wait all night for it?"

"Oh, Doctor, I didn't see you come on the ward. I'll get it," the nurse said.

When she got back with the equipment, the nursing supervisor accompanied her.

As I stooped over the patient and inserted the NG tube, I shouted, "This comatose girl with half a brain is smarter than all the nurses in the rehab unit combined!"

There was dead silence on the ward as I stormed off, but silence was not how I would describe my meeting at 7 a.m. The nursing supervisor wrote me up, and the assistant resident director called me as soon as he heard about the incident.

The director of the program was a kindly old physician who could not yell if he wanted to, but his assistant, referred to as Dr. Hitler, made up for any meanness needed. The short conversation went something like this:

Hitler: *Do you like being an intern here?*

Elkmoss: *Yes, sir.*

Hitler: *Do you know that it is one heck of a lot easier to replace an intern, particularly an obnoxious one like you, than it is a nurse?*

Elkmoss: *Not really, sir.*

Hitler: *If I ever hear of you even looking cross-eyed at a nurse at this hospital again, you'll be out on your ear. Do you understand?*

Elkmoss: *Yes, sir.*

I learned the lesson well and behaved the rest of the year. I was called to rehab a couple more times, but I was a much kinder and gentler soul. Towards the end of my internship year, the rehab unit called me. They knew I was not on duty, but wanted to show me something.

When I got to the annex, the nurses took me to the little girl's room. She was sitting up, chatting and giggling with her mother. She still had marked left sided weakness but was clearly on her way to recovery. The nurses explained that after seven months of a coma, she suddenly came out of it and was like this—a joy to her family and nurses.

It was quite an internship year, and I learned a lot. One of the most the most important lessons I received—that of respecting nurses—was rendered by a fourteen-year-old diabetic girl with a severe head injury.

Several years later and after starting private practice, I married a nurse. I told people then that I thought it was the only way I could get my orders followed on the ward, but anyone who is married to a nurse knows better.

Recently, I was asked to testify at a hearing conducted by the state legislature to look into the causes of the nursing shortage as well as the shortage of health care workers in general. The chair of the committee was an older lady and I was trying to explain that if the legislature did not make improvements in the climate of medicine, we were in danger of losing a lot of physicians. In passing, I told her that I had married a nurse from Moss State and since I could never convince her to move, there was no danger of losing me.

The chair interrupted and said, "And marrying that nurse, young man, was the best decision you ever made!"

I agreed.

CHAPTER 48
PARKINSON'S DISEASE

I think all us doctors want to make a diagnosis that saves or spectacularly improves the life of a patient. Those occasions probably arise more often in surgery than in neurology, but I seem to recall one set of patients, those with Parkinson's disease, that get the closest to generating that feeling for me.

One of the first Parkinson patients I ever diagnosed was a fellow in the psych ward at the Veterans Administration Hospital (VAH) that was staffed by our residency program at Southern Fungus Medical University. Having to see a VA psych patient for us was dreaded just about as much as being called in to see the chairman of the department for some mistake we had made. Since I was a new resident and certainly not wanting to be chewed out by the chairman for neglect of duty, I drudged over to the VAH to see Henry.

Henry was in his late sixties and loved to bowl. He had been in a bowling league for more than thirty years and several months earlier had been kicked off his team when his scores had dropped significantly. This just destroyed the man and he ended up sulking around the house for a month or so until his wife could not stand it any more. She dragged him down to the VA hospital and he was admitted to the psych ward for melancholy. He had been in the VAH with that diagnosis for another month. They had plied poor Henry with every antidepressant therapy they could think of, but all to no avail.

It was then that some bright psych resident requested a neurology consult, and I was the lucky one picked to see him. While watching Henry shuffle down the hall to the exam room, I recognized all the symptoms of Parkinson's disease. After starting him on medicines, Henry dramatically improved. He was quickly discharged from the hospital (which would be therapeutic by itself), and by the time I saw him back in the outpatient clinic six weeks later, he had been reinstated on his beloved bowling team and a happy veteran. I ended up following his bowling averages for the rest of the three years I was there. Every time his average slipped a little, I just upped his Parkinson's medicine.

My successes in managing Parkinson's disease have not always been appreciated by my patients, however. Take, for instance, Myrtle. She had suffered from arthritis for many years. When she had become practically immobile, her primary care doctor succeeded in having her admitted to a rehab hospital where she continued to do poorly. The rehab physician thought it was just the arthritis that kept her from improving. Several months after Myrtle had been admitted to the facility, a family physician friend of mine, Bob, covering for the vacationing rehab specialist, asked me to see her. She, of course, was suffering from Parkinson's disease and had a dramatic response to medicine.

Six weeks later, Myrtle with her sister easily walked, not shuffled, into my office for a follow-up appointment. This feat was accomplished, mind you, after nearly eight months of living in a wheelchair. I asked Myrtle how she was doing and she said in a depressed voice, "Oh, I don't know. I just don't feel right. Can you do anything for me?"

Myrtle's sister just had a fit, reminding her sister that she had not even been able to walk until starting on the Parkinson's medicine.

Over the years following that, Myrtle had a rich, full life in spite of her difficulties with Parkinson's disease. She taught me an important point. Even though Parkinson's disease is a movement disorder, just addressing the movement difficulties was not enough when managing this disease.

And the lack of appreciation for my success in treating Parkinson's disease extended to my own colleagues as well. Eleanor Hill was a neat lady in her early eighties when she shuffled into my office after slowing down considerably over the previous six months. She had been a very energetic lady and the slowness was really frustrating her.

After explaining that I thought she had Parkinson's disease and starting her on some medicines, I made arrangements to see her back in six weeks. A month later, however, I was consulted by an orthopedist, Dr. Bones, to see her in the hospital. Seems that after several weeks on medicines for the Parkinson's disease, she had felt so good she jumped on her granddaughter's bicycle and rode around the neighborhood. Unfortunately, she fell and broke a leg.

When I ran into Dr. Bones who had spent the previous night operating on her, he was indignant. "What the hell were you thinking about when you let an eighty-year-old lady ride a bicycle?" Bones said as he rushed down the hall, leaving me in bewilderment.

I never did let him know that I was really very satisfied with my diagnostic skills and treatment of Eleanor. Like many orthopedists, he was a big, athletic kind of guy who probably would have broken *my* leg if he knew what I was thinking.

CHAPTER 49
INTERNATIONAL SPEAKER

There are some studies that show standing up in public to talk ranks first on the list of what people fear the most (with fear of death listed as third). In my case, fear of public speaking is second to fear of losing my slides, or nowadays, an electronic outage during a PowerPoint presentation.

Years ago, I received an invitation to give a talk in the Bahamas and was initially thrilled. After all, the company provided me accommodations at Paradise Island and a round trip plane ticket. I could even put down on my resumé that I was an international speaker. But as the time arrived to make the big trip, the fear of losing my slides (there were two carousels, not just one) became paramount in my mind. I even went so far as to make a second copy (at an enormous cost).

With one set of slides in my checked baggage and another with me, I set off from Moss State to Miami where I was to take a small "puddle jumper" to Nassau. (The island was not large enough to support big jets.) The airlines had just started a policy of overbooking flights and my flight was overbooked by two people. They started by offering a $50 travel voucher and a flight to Nassau that would leave three hours later, around 9 p.m. After a couple minutes, they made the offer again and someone gave up their seat. When no one else was interested in the later flight, they kept upping the price. Finally, just minutes before the flight was to take off, they raised the price to $400 and dinner. I decided to take the offer. After all, my tickets were free, the $400 was a big bonus, and I could afford to get to Paradise Island late.

The other passenger who had taken the offer earlier was a Hollywood attorney whose firm worked for Merv Griffin, the owner of Paradise Island. John was a very friendly fellow and we had dinner together (at the airline's expense) while we waited for the next flight. He was a little ticked that he had accepted the $50 instead of $400, but nonetheless, we got along quite nicely. He had made the trip to Paradise Island as many as four times a year conducting business for his client, so he knew his way around Nassau.

While in flight, the conversation turned to more mundane things such as Bahamian beer. John pointed out that Kalik beer, the national brew, was perhaps the finest in the world. We shared a cab from the airport to Paradise Island and while passing through what looked like back roads to the resort, John told the cab driver to pull into a little store where we could buy some beer rather than pay the exorbitant prices they would charge at the hotel.

I was a little reluctant, but John pushed me into the store. We looked around and each bought a six-pack of Kalik. After paying a surly shopkeeper, we stepped outside to get back into the cab. It was gone!

My life flashed before me. The missing cab had my entire luggage, including both sets of slides. I was destroyed, but John was nonplused. He repeatedly said such things like cab drivers taking customers' luggage never happened there. He suggested that the driver just went off to get gas while waiting for us.

After ten minutes (that seemed like hours) even John gave up and went back in and told the store owner. He came out and asked us for the cab number and name of the driver. We, of course, did not even know the name of the cab company, let alone any other details.

"You idiots," the store owner said. "Wait here for a couple more minutes. If he doesn't show, come back inside and I'll call the police."

We waited and waited with John repeatedly saying that this kind of thing never happened in the Bahamas. I had already sunk into deep despair, standing on the street with a six-pack of Kalik beer in hand.

After twenty more minutes (or was it hours?) John finally had enough and started to go inside the store. All of a sudden, however, the cab came driving up and screeched to a stop.

"Ay, mon," he said in a thick Bahamian accent, "me ain' leave you. I go to come back."

Both John and I collided, scrambling to get in the back seat. It turned out that the driver had noticed a leak in one of his tires. Since his brother ran a car repair shop just down the street, he took off to get the tire fixed. It took longer than he thought it would.

I made it successfully to Paradise Island with my slides, luggage, and the six-pack of Kalik beer. The following day, my talk went quite nicely (thank you very much) and I even ran into John on the floor of the casino that evening. We were cordial enough, but the whole experience just soured me even more against lawyers (as if I needed more reasons to dread that profession).

I also drank a couple of the Kalik beers while I was in Nassau and even brought two bottles home. It might be a very good beer, and if you blindfolded and served me some today, I probably would tell you it is okay. But frankly, it brings up such terrible memories (such as a brush-with-worse-than-death feeling), that I have no interest in ever drinking the brew again.

CHAPTER 50
HOSPITAL PARKING TICKETS

In all the hospital studies of patient satisfaction, staff efficiency, and medical staff needs that I have filled out (seems like I have seen a million of these surveys), no one has asked my opinion about parking tickets. It is a particularly important subject these days because hospitals undergo a lot of changes. When they do, administrators tend to forget about the security department. Security guards then start acting like boy scouts without adult leadership. Next, parking tickets flood the windshields of the cars of the medical staff, nurses, patients and their families.

I recognize that a big security issue of older hospitals is parking. Particularly at inner city hospitals, the security department, not only needs to make sure no one is parked in the wrong place, but protect the staff on long journeys to and from their vehicles.

When I first started working at a community hospital, I thought that my parking problems would be over. Not so. I arrived at the first joint medical staff meeting a little late, and the only parking place I could find was the CEO's spot. Interestingly, it was empty because the CEO skipped the meeting. Shows how much contempt he had for the medical staff. In addition, it raises an issue about lack of parking spaces for doctors because administrators take up all the spots. But that is another subject for another time. When I came out of the meeting, an over eager security policeman had put a ticket on my windshield. In retrospect, it was probably a fairly benign warning that I had parked in the wrong spot, but it ticked me off.

Coincidentally, I had an orientation meeting with the CEO the following day. I asked if it was part of the orientation of new doctors to give them parking tickets. He first tried to justify it but quickly agreed to take care of the ticket when I started laughing.

I did not really have any more difficulties with parking tickets until years later when Moss Community Hospital underwent some changes. The CEO at the time (two executive officers later) was showing me how the construction was going. I asked him if he was going to have a fancy parking place. He told me early in his career he had learned that administrators should never have marked parking places.

"That way, no one can tell if you are working or not," he pointed out.

I might not have been able to tell if he was working, but I certainly could tell his security police were. The hospital improvements took place in three stages over a two-year period. Each stage was accompanied by two moves of the designated doctor parking areas and most times these were accomplished by notifying the physicians several days late—or never. I managed to collect ten parking ticket "reminders" during these moves. Most of my colleagues also got tickets and just tore them up (adding more litter to the construction), but I kept mine. The departure of the CEO came shortly after the grand opening of the new hospital facility, and the medical staff presented him with a going away present consisting of all the tickets I had collected during his tenure.

Those tickets were just reminders, so tearing them up could be therapeutic to a disturbed physician and had no consequences. Regular tickets issued by hospital security should also have no meaning except to irritate people. At least that is what I thought until my partner, Kildeer, got called into the hospital to see an emergency consult on a Saturday night. He pulled into the outpatient oncology parking lot that was completely empty. When he came out, there was a ticket waving on his windshield noting that he had illegally parked in a handicap spot. Usually, he just tears up tickets, but this time he went around to the ER where he actually found the culprit who wrote the tag and accosted him. After Kildeer pointed out that there were absolutely no other cars in the parking lot and that there are a zillion things security could be doing such as preventing laptop computers, TVs, and even scales from being stolen from the hospital, he threw the ticket in the security guard's lap. As Kildeer dramatically stormed off, the security man pointed out, because of an arrangement with the Swampville police, that the ticket represented a city violation and he would have to take care of it down at city hall!

The story has a happy ending because the following Monday morning, Kildeer talked to the head of security and had the ticket held. (Seems that the security office works a lot slower on the weekends. I guess that is the time to steal laptops and things, too. Are you criminals out there listening?)

The message that needed to be delivered to the administration, though, was that no tickets should be given to anyone at the hospital. Give warnings maybe (even those can be overdone), but never tickets, and particularly not "real" tickets. Citations only irritate and enrage people like patients, patients' families, staff, and physicians alike—all the people the hospital should want to keep happy. Furthermore, even if the ticket is validated, the city would get the fine, not the hospital. It was all summarized by Kildeer when he said, "Giving hospital security people the privilege to write city tickets is like giving Barney Fife real bullets!"

CHAPTER 51
PROJECT EXODUS

With the hospitals in the area trying to make doctors computer-literate and initiating systems for reporting, charting, and even ordering online, I thought it was time for Elkmoss to comment on the subject. One particular program is called Project Exodus. I assume the name was chosen because the hospital is trying to lead doctors out of the dark ages into modern medicine. Unlike my very computer-literate kids, it is a painful experience to learn new things. Even so, I anticipate practicing medicine for the foreseeable future, so I am trying to adjust to the system changes, attend computer classes, and not gripe too much in the process.

One of my biggest problems is the need for numerous passwords. When combined with all the passwords required to access online organizations, journals, and shopping, it gets unmanageable. To simplify things I tried to use the same password for everything, but the hospital has frustrated me by requiring changes in passwords every ninety days. Even if I could remember my user ID numbers, constantly changing all the passwords would require an enormous amount of time.

One day, I received a letter announcing the start of a program called "ReadyAccess" which would allow me to access hospital stuff from my home computer (issuing me another user ID and password to remember). When I got home, I went online to set up the program. Halfway through the setup procedure I got a message that the "server is unavailable."

Following the instructions, I called the "Help Line." After some thirty hours (well, it seemed like thirty hours), the lady on the other end said, "Gee, my server is unavailable, too. Do you want me call back later when it is working?"

"No," I said. "I'll just call back tomorrow when I can waste some more time on this."

The next day when I tried to get online, I could not even connect, let alone try to set up, ReadyAccess. So I called the cable company that provides both my high-speed internet access and TV service. After another fifteen hours of waiting (it seemed like they were twice as fast as the hospital help line), a pleasant lady started asking me to look at a bunch of lights on the modem box. As I scooted my chair back, it caught on a cord and flipped me to the floor. Meanwhile, I continued to talk on the phone like nothing had happened. I already sounded like a computer illiterate (which I am), and I did not want to seem like a total klutz (which I am also).

Then she finally asked me if my TV cable was working. It was out, so she told me she would transfer me to the folks that handled cable problems—disconnecting me altogether!

Two days later and even a trip by the cable guy, I finally was connected again. After I showed the cable guy to the door, I eagerly accessed the internet but still could not get linked to ReadyAccess. I called the hospital technical support number, and they finally gave up after about an hour of trying to talk me through the hook up. They told me someone else would be calling to help fix the problem.

No one called. The following week, two weeks after trying to get connected to ReadyAccess, I griped at hospital administration. Not only did the IT folks contact me, they actually sent a technician to my house that afternoon to personally install my ReadyAccess.

Although he looked like he was still in high school and took more than an hour to get me connected (thus making me feel a little better about my incompetence with computers), he successfully had me online. I was actually feeling a little grateful (emphasis on *little*) for his help and was thanking him when he looked up and saw "Dr. Herman J. Elkmoss" on a plaque.

"Oh," he said, "are you a doctor?"

"Well, yes I am," I said thinking it strange that a hospital technician would not have known he was being sent out to a physician's house.

Then, while shaking my hand, he asked, "Do you still practice?"

If I had any good thoughts about computers, or hospitals for that matter, they dissipated at that point. I have no reason to believe I will be "set free" by Project Exodus and I certainly am not convinced that the system will be Ready Accessible to me. I have come to the conclusion that we just ought to move on to *Revelations* and Project Armageddon!

CHAPTER 52
MISSING PIECES

Just this year I was fortunate to celebrate twenty-five years of practice. In looking back (which was restricted somewhat because Mrs. Elkmoss does not like to think she is married to an old man), there is a great deal of professional satisfaction in practicing medicine in one place for an extended length of time. In the residency program, I would rarely see the long-term effects of an illness on patients and families. Now I do, and every once in a while, I even get to see patients I saw as children, now grown up with families of their own. It is quite an experience, but there are also a couple irritants.

One problem is a phenomenon of getting attached to equipment, then not being able to get replacement parts. For instance, I have a reflex hammer that I bought when I was an intern, thirty years ago. Several years ago, the tip finally wore off and I needed a replacement. The equipment company I bought it from had long since disappeared, so I was out of luck.

Thanks to the internet, however, and several hours of research (I probably spent more time investigating reflex hammer tips than any complicated disease), I finally found the replacement part. I was so pleased with my find that I ordered three sets of replacements. Now I am fixed for another seventy-five years of practice!

My concern over the inability of getting spare parts was emphasized the other day as I was leaving the hospital after a long day. In the relatively large hospital parking lot near my car, I found a white plastic earpiece for a stethoscope. Normally I would have put it in my pocket, intending to ask around the hospital if anyone had lost an earpiece. Then I would leave it in some drawer at home until Mrs. Elkmoss found it and used it as evidence that I was the biggest packrat in the world. (She does not need any more proof to verify her point.)

Those thoughts went through my head as I stood there looking at the earpiece. After all, the odds of me finding who owned the earpiece were next to impossible. So, in a moment of sheer rational thought (rare as it might be), I put the earpiece back on the ground. Mrs. Elkmoss had no idea why I seemed so righteous when I got home.

Early the next morning, I was in the doctors' lounge at the hospital and ran into Dr. Elder, the oldest practicing physician on staff. He is a throwback to what I envision a doctor should be. He still is probably the first physician to make rounds in the morning and the last to leave the hospital in the evening. He even makes house calls, and, if I think twenty-five years of practice is rewarding, Dr Elder's almost fifty years is phenomenal.

So there was Dr. Elder whom I rarely see these days (since I am not usually in the hospital making rounds at midnight), his stethoscope hanging on his neck with a white earpiece missing! When I pointed it out, he said he knew it was missing (I could only imagine what kind of ENT problems it would have caused if he had put it in his ear), but he said he was frustrated at not being able to get a replacement and so used to wearing his stethoscope that he just put it on that morning without thinking.

I told him I saw an earpiece the day before in the parking lot and we both went out to see if we could find it. The parking lot was practically empty, being early in the morning, and sure enough, we found Elder's missing earpiece.

I have not run into Dr. Elder lately (I guess I need to stay in the hospital a little longer to see him), but I have taken out my favorite stethoscope and made sure the earpieces are tight. I also have briefly thought of telling Mrs. Elkmoss of my experience, but I am afraid she would just turn it around to prove that I really do not need to be a packrat after all. I do know that in the midst of all the little irritants of practicing medicine, I was lucky enough to have this success.

CHAPTER 53
RETIREMENT

As a young physician just starting out in practice, I gave little thought to retirement or what some of my colleagues have referred to as the "end game." I do not think I am alone in that apathy. I see older physicians who practice long after they should have retired and many more just do not know what to do with themselves after they lay down their stethoscopes.

For example, one physician I know was a very active and innovative doctor. In his mid-fifties he suffered a mild heart attack. Normally you would expect him to take that as a message to slow down, get control of his physical condition and diet, and continue practice as he certainly had a lot more to contribute to medicine.

Unfortunately, one of his sons was an insurance representative and had sold his father something like $2 million worth of disability insurance. If he went back to practice, even part-time, he would have to forego all those benefits. After a couple months of agonizing over his fate, he decided to retire and take the millions of dollars. That left an enormous void in this very accomplished man's life and he seemed like a lost soul. He eventually took a prolonged vacation to Alaska and, somewhere between Juno and Fairbanks, had an epiphany. When he returned he became heavily involved in what was called transitional medicine programs that helped physicians change careers. When I last saw him he seemed very content with life.

There are other physicians that decide to retire early, but after several months or a year, get bored, realize that they are happiest practicing medicine, and return to doctoring.

Several years ago, I decided to not let retirement issues come at me by surprise like it happens to many others. After all, in many ways the practice of medicine has changed considerably in the last thirty years. Managed care, insurance company problems, lawsuits, and many more issues have often made it an increasing challenge to be happy "saving lives and stamping out disease."

While attending a conference in Florida, I had the opportunity to visit an old friend who was a retired physician. He had practiced in Moss State for more than thirty years. When his mother-in-law could no longer live in her Florida condominium, he bought it and moved in. After a couple of years of living in Moss State six months a year and Florida the rest of the time, he just moved South full time. He was kind enough to take me to lunch at his golf club.

Over a great salad (Mrs. Elkmoss always wants me to eat good foods, particularly on vacations), I could not resist asking him about some of the issues I should be thinking about when I considered retirement.

The old fellow thought about the question for a minute and then raised his fork to point at the rest of the people in the grill. "See this club?" he said. "The average waiting time for folks to become members is ten years. So if you think you want to retire in ten years and join a club like this, you better get your application in now."

I let that profound statement settle for a couple minutes while I chewed my veggies. (I do not know why I was eating such health food. Mrs. Elkmoss was back home more than a thousand miles away.) I thought that for all his experience practicing medicine as well as retiring, I might just gain a little more profound information.

"Is there anything else you could share with me about retirement that might help?"

"Well, yes," he said. "You know that while you are in practice, trying to be a good father, husband and doctor, you don't get out on the golf course as much as you would like? You tend to think that when you retire and get a chance to play more often, your handicap will drop. Well, it doesn't."

I am still in practice, my golf game sucks, and I am not sure what criteria to use to quit the practice of medicine. Perhaps I should put in my request to become a member at that Florida golf course and, when I get accepted, make that the time to retire.

SECTION III
LIFE IN GENERAL

The key to longevity is to have a chronic incurable disease and take good care of it.

Dr. Oliver Wendell Holmes

CHAPTER 54
FATHERS-IN-LAW

Dear Abby often dispenses advice concerning how wives should deal with mothers-in-law, but rarely (if at all) have I seen any advice on husbands dealing with their fathers-in-law. I must say that Mrs. Elkmoss's father, Bumpy (as his grandchildren have named him), has been ideal. Among his many talents, he is a master mechanic as well as a general "fix-it" man. If I ever have a car problem or house repair difficulty, I call Bumpy.

If I did not appreciate his abilities at first, Mrs. Elkmoss has made sure I know how reliable her father is. Every time something goes wrong in our house, particularly when I am in the middle of something else like saving lives and stamping out disease and cannot help her just then, she just says, "Oh, that's okay. I'll just call my dad!"

Bumpy is always aware of my male ego, however, and even when he quickly adjusted the drain of our bathroom sink that I could not figure out for months, he kindly said in front of his daughter, "That's a pretty tricky knob. No wonder you had so much trouble with it. It sure isn't like the sinks we used to have."

I think Bumpy appreciated my incompetence with home maintenance early on. Perhaps he first understood the night I asked for his daughter's hand in marriage.

After the future Mrs. Elkmoss agreed to marry me, we thought it would be a great idea to invite my future in-laws to dinner at my house. Then, in the course of the meal, I would formally ask her father for permission to marry his daughter. I obviously wanted to make the evening rather special, so I took great efforts to clean up the house. Since it was summer and I had a nice deck, I wanted to put up torches that supposedly keep mosquitoes away and have a candlelight dinner outside.

While cleaning the deck the Saturday morning of the dinner, I noticed it was starting to peel. I quickly rushed off to the hardware store and told the clerk my problem. He came up with a paint that would dry quickly, within four hours. What I failed to appreciate was that the paint I had bought was a water-based paint, and the paint on the deck was oil-based.

I had the deck all painted by noon, more than seven hours before my future in-laws would arrive, so I spent the rest of the day cleaning the house. Every once in a while, particularly after the guaranteed-four-hours-to-dry time had expired, I checked the deck and it was still sticky. Finally, with just a half hour before my future in-laws arrived and the deck still sticky, I cancelled the outdoor plans and set up dinner on the dinette table that overlooked the deck.

Things went well, but unfortunately the sun had not set before we sat down to eat. My future mother-in-law looked out on the deck, thought it was very nice, and proceeded to open the door to walk out.

"STOP," I shouted while carrying over a basket of rolls I had just taken from the oven. You would have thought she had stolen the roast beef I was getting ready to serve.

The future Mrs. Elkmoss, not knowing of my blunder with the paint (I was still trying to impress her with my many talents and I had not told her about my stupidity), told her mother she certainly could walk out on the porch.

I had to confess my error and it was then I could tell my future father-in-law knew what an incompetent person I really was. As we sat down to dinner, however, he quickly pointed out to the ladies that, "The new paints are pretty tricky and not like the paints we used to have."

The rest of the evening went spectacularly well, however. During dessert when I asked for his daughter's hand in marriage, I thought Bumpy was going to choke. I do not know if it was because he was surprised or was worried about my abilities to take care of his daughter, but he quickly gave his approval. I think he knew then that by approving the marriage, he was going to be spending the bulk of his retirement years training an incompetent son-in-law.

And he has done a fine job, if I do say so. It has been at least a week since Mrs. Elkmoss has said, "Well if you won't fix it, I'll just call my dad!"

CHAPTER 55
CAR LOCKS

When I was little and taking family trips, Mother Elkmoss would religiously make sure we all locked the car doors. When we had young kids of our own, Mrs. Elkmoss would also make sure the doors were secure, and she felt vindicated with all the carjacking stories she read about. Our kids are all grown now, but she still prefers making sure the doors are locked when we go anywhere. Recently, however, I have noticed a little irritation with our new car that automatically locks the doors when put in gear. She has not figured out how to override the lock, so when she wants to run back into the house for something she forgot (which is frequently), she has to wait until I put the car in park. If I do not do it within three nanoseconds after she tries unsuccessfully to open the door, I get a dirty look.

Although my opinion has never been sought on the matter (neither Mother Elkmoss or Mrs. Elkmoss really cared what I thought of locking car doors), I was rather neutral. As a good son and later, husband, I kept quiet on the subject. It is not that I did not think about it. After all, I did not want to be carjacked either. Somehow or other, though, if someone was waiving a gun at me through a locked car door and told me he was going to blow my head off if I did not let him in, I think I might be tempted to open the door. Then too, if I was ever in an accident and unconscious with a fire threatening to engulf me, I think I would have wanted the doors unlocked so someone could save my life. I do not like the vision of becoming a crispy critter while waiting for the Jaws of Life.

These arguments clearly would not sway Mrs. Elkmoss, but they have passed through my mind on occasion when I am told to lock the car doors. I also think a colleague of mine, Dr. Beak, also had the same indoctrination I had. Beak, in his early forties, had an active solo practice. He also had an irregular heartbeat. One day, he attended an all-day medical conference at Moss State University. About halfway home, while traveling on the interstate with all his car doors locked, he started feeling dizzy. He pulled over to the side of the road just before losing consciousness.

Fortunately, just behind him was an off-duty policeman who had observed Beak weaving off the road. He actually thought Beak was drunk or something and pulled up right behind him. Beak had gone into a full cardiac arrest and was having a convulsion when the policeman got to Beak's car.

The locked door obviously presented a problem, but the quick thinking policeman saw a brick on the side of the road, quickly broke the window, and was able to pull Beak out. He was well trained in CPR and, as luck would have it, there was an ICU nurse in the car behind him. Not only was she able to expertly help the resuscitation, she had a cell phone and was able to call for an evacuation helicopter. Literally within minutes Beak had been transported and admitted to Moss State University Hospital.

Unfortunately, Beak had sustained significant anoxic brain injury and, although his cardiac condition had been stabilized, he remained in a coma. Mrs. Beak recalled bitterly that the neurologist consulting on the case had painted a very poor prognosis for recovery, but she was adamant that everything be done for her husband. To everyone's surprise, he recovered consciousness several days later and went on to make a full recovery. His physicians placed a rather recently developed implantable cardioverter-defibrillator (ICD) device and he was able to resume practice about six months after his cardiac arrest.

Prior to the experience, Beak had been a somewhat obnoxious person. His constant complaining and rudeness to patients, nurses, and colleagues was quite well-known. Now, he was a grateful person and set about successfully reestablishing his practice. He even had a big party to recognize the off duty policeman and nurse who had been so instrumental in saving his life.

Several years later, Beak's ICD device went off while he was seeing a patient. It was a signal that it was time to quit practice. He is now happily active in the community, participating in church and service organizations, and is one of the stellar contributors to the city. I ran into him at a medical society meeting and could not help asking if he still locked his car door on trips.

"Certainly," he said immediately. "It makes me feel very secure."

I guess Beak is statistically correct in locking his car doors while traveling. The odds are higher that you will be carjacked than have a cardiac arrest, so I have resigned myself to follow the insistence of Mrs. Elkmoss and keep my doors locked.

CHAPTER 56
DUCKS UNLIMITED

After I married Mrs. Elkmoss, her father, Bumpy, as his grandkids later named him, started taking me to the annual Ducks Unlimited banquet. He never said, but I believe he was somewhat disappointed that his new son-in-law cared very little about the manly sport of hunting. Perhaps he thought my exposure to Ducks Unlimited might stir up some interest. He stirred up my interest all right, but not in shooting birds.

The crowning event at the banquet was an auction of various hunting items including two Ducks Unlimited "Limited Edition" shotguns. When the first shotgun was offered, folks were really reluctant to bid. Finally, to the surprise of our table, Bumpy chirped in with a bid of $400. He won (or should I say, lost). His other buddies asked him if he was out of his mind; his wife would kill him for such a frivolous expense. Meanwhile, the auctioneer trotted out another shotgun. Pretty soon, Bumpy bid $600 and bought the gun!

As we were waiting to pay for the shotguns at the end of the banquet, my father-in-law explained that the shotguns were worth more than $1,000 each, and he had just made a killing. I agreed with him, but the killing part was going to be when my mother-in-law found out. And the more I thought about it, Mrs. Elkmoss would not think too kindly about me letting her father get in so much trouble. That would translate into major problems for me, so I offered to buy one of them.

The maneuver did not save either one of us from the wrath of Mrs. Elkmoss or her mother. All it did was deprive me of $400 (I took the cheaper one) and stuck me with gun with which I had no idea what to do. The following week I explained all this to Dr. Bob, a family physician who lived across the street from me. He was an avid sportsman and decided to take me duck hunting. After all, it was a Ducks Unlimited shotgun, so I might as well try to shoot some "limited" ducks with it.

What Bob failed to tell me was the great risk to my life such an outing would become. We had to get up at an ungodly hour in the morning to travel to some remote marsh in the middle of nowhere to wade in water at nearly freezing temperatures. He made me put on chest-high waders and then gave me specific instructions to stay put while he wandered around a pond in the middle of the marsh, stringing duck decoys. It was pitch black and all I could appreciate was some splashing around as Bob placed his decoys. I was standing approximately twenty feet from shore with cold water up to my waist when I made the mistake of trying to move a little. I stepped into some sort of a hole. The water rushed into my waders, and I was splashing around, drowning.

Luckily, Bob was nearby and saved me, dragging my drenched, cold body to the edge of the marsh. The only bright spot was that I had left the shotgun on shore and did not lose it.

It took me a while to recover from the trauma of duck hunting, but by the next season, Bob had convinced me to go grouse hunting with him. It would be during the daylight hours. We would just be traipsing around the woods and communing with nature. There would be no water exposure unless I was dumb enough to jump into a creek or something.

Moss State has hunting regulations limiting shotguns to three shells instead of the five they normally hold. I did not know that rule and put all five shells in the gun as Bob and I took off on our safari. We walked all day long and never saw anything that resembled a grouse. I was a little (very) frustrated with the whole hunting thing. When I finally heard the rustling of feathers that Bob told me would be the sound of a grouse, I was excited. Flying away from me was the only grouse I had ever recognized. Although it was miles away, I started firing my shotgun, all five shots, and naturally missed the bird.

Just as I finished emptying my gun, another grouse flew up in front of me. If I had enough sense I could have hit it with the butt of my Ducks Unlimited shotgun. As it was, I had fired all my ammo, and all I could do was watch and listen as the bird flew away. Bob tells me that grouse do not cackle, but I am pretty sure this one did. Bob also explained to me that if the Department of Natural Resources had seen me fire off five shots, they would have confiscated my shotgun, his car, and fined us both severely.

By then Bob should have had enough of trying to make me into a hunter. But no. He was convinced that with my deficient aptitude, I would appreciate pheasant hunting. He eventually organized a six-man group to go to South Dakota, supposedly the finest pheasant-hunting place in the world. By the time we could free up our schedules to make the trip, however, it was three weeks into the season and all the pheasants apparently had been shot or left the state. The only thing we saw all day long trudging through cornfields was a rabbit the size of a small deer. I really would have been satisfied with the trip, but Bob had to complain to his partner's father-in-law (here's another father-in-law, Father-in-Law #2) where we were staying. He took us out to a field guaranteed to have pheasants.

All seven of us walked along in a row, but there were only six hunters since Father-in-Law #2 was not carrying a gun. He was surprised that there were no pheasants. I was walking beside him explaining that I did not think there were any pheasants in South Dakota when one took off in front of us. It rose just to the left of our row and flew left to right in plain view of everyone. We all fired at the pheasant and missed all twenty shots. Now someone might be counting and figure that with three shots apiece, also the restriction in South Dakota, there should have been only eighteen shots fired. Where did the other two shots come from? My Ducks Unlimited shotgun, of course. I again had put five rounds in my chamber. With all the fireworks, however, no one seemed to notice my stupidity. Father-in-Law #2 did notice the poor shooting. He just shook his head and said, "You boys will have to do better than that!"

We did not do any better than that, and we did not see another pheasant the rest of the trip. We had to console ourselves back in Moss State by telling all our friends that there was just one pheasant in all of South Dakota.

Dr. Bob and Bumpy have finally given up on making a hunter out of me. For the last couple of years, I have not even been invited to the Ducks Unlimited banquet. I do have a Ducks Unlimited etching in my office they used to give everyone who attended the banquet. It leaves the impression that I am a sportsman or something—with the emphasis on "something."

CHAPTER 57
CHEESEBURGERS IN PARADISE

While going through the rigors of medical school, internship, and residency, I often took refuge in listening to Jimmy Buffett songs. He seemed a laid-back kind of guy and his songs about places like "Margaritaville" were just what I needed to hear after finishing a thirty-six hour stint in the hospital. His popular song, "Cheeseburger in Paradise," particularly seemed to cement my understanding of American culture and what McDonald's was all about.

In private practice, my interest in the music of Jimmy Buffett gradually evolved into an interest in the investment strategies of Warren Buffett, but my love of cheeseburgers continued as strong as ever. It was so intense that after gaining forty extra pounds, I had to reduce my appreciation of cheeseburgers to just having a picture hanging in my study.

Meanwhile, the cheeseburger as well as the related fat food craze continued to grow (so to speak) until now we face an obesity crisis in the United States. So war on cheeseburgers has been declared, and one of the weapons gaining popularity is bariatric surgery. I am not really sure of the philosophy behind this surgery, but it has gained a lot of momentum. Seems to me that we are doing elective surgery on folks who are much higher operative risks for a disorder not necessarily caused by an anatomical problem.

Philosophy aside, however, there is reason enough to try to do something to help a morbidly obese person. But for me, the difficulties with bariatric surgery have tarnished Jimmy's "Cheeseburger in Paradise."

The other day, Mrs. Elkmoss came home from teaching a group of nursing students. We did not get a chance to talk much as we were rushing to get to a party, but I noticed every once in a while she would just break out laughing. Finally, when we were in the car by ourselves, she explained that her nursing students that day helped prepare patients for bariatric surgery. She had heard a commotion in hall and came up to the group of pupils. It seems that in cleaning up a 450-plus-pound lady for surgery, a student had lifted up a big roll of belly fat and discovered a cheeseburger—with a bite out of it!

The ensuing discussion regarding the discovered cheeseburger (referred to as the "DC" so as not to violate governmental rules of disclosing medical information) centered around speculation as to how that poor lady had lost her cheeseburger. One might have suspected it had just fallen out of a bag or something, but there was a bite taken out of it. That means she had to have had her hands on that burger and it just got away somehow. For the rest of the day, Mrs. Elkmoss would think about that cheeseburger and break out laughing. I still sometimes catch her giggling about it.

Jimmy Buffett further ruined my concept of "Cheeseburger in Paradise" by suing several people for using the title for their restaurants. Apparently he wanted a chain of restaurants with that name. So here was a man whom I thought set an example of being a carefree kind of a guy that is in reality a hardheaded businessman. Maybe I should write Jimmy a note with an idea for a another song entitled "Lost Cheeseburger in Paradise."

CHAPTER 58
THE COLD STATE OF MOSS

Even though I am from the North, I have always been a warm weather fan. Unfortunately, Mrs. Elkmoss has remained uninterested in having anything to do with the South. Every time I mention something about a place where it is warm all year, she says she would miss the four seasons. I usually counter that in the three years I spent at Southern Fungus Medical University (SFMU), I never saw a snowflake and never missed it.

When we were first married, I realized the resistance Mrs. Elkmoss had for the South, so I waited and waited until just the right medical conference came along for me to showcase warm-weather living. Finally after a couple of years, SFMU had a conference in the middle of October. We stayed at a beach condo for a week while I attended the meetings and she lounged around in the sand. The weather was perfect, mid-seventies with no rain. With confidence that I had made some progress in my quest for southern living, we boarded the plane back to Moss State.

As I leaned back in my seat, I said to Mrs. Elkmoss, "Well, dear, what do you think of the South?"

"Oh," she casually said, "it was too humid. My hair got all limp!"

It was a rather depressing flight home as I knew if she did not like that week in the South, she would never agree to a Southern existence of any sort. So I have patiently waited and waited, and I think there is an opportunity I might get my wish after all. Of course this opportunity has come at enormous cost to my reputation as a great diagnostician, let alone a caring husband.

Several years ago, Mrs. Elkmoss's grandparents, in their mid-eighties, moved to a house across the street from us. It gave them a little more comfort having an obsessive-compulsive nurse-granddaughter nearby. Every Monday evening Mrs. Elkmoss would go across the street to get her grandparents' medicines set for the week.

One very cold evening in February, I came out of the study (the cave as the rest of the family refers to it) to go to bed. It was 10 p.m. and past my usual bedtime, so I went upstairs to put my coffee cup in the dishwasher (like a dutiful husband) and also closed the garage door that was open, thinking that one of the kids had forgotten to close it. I then went to bed and was sound asleep in our downstairs bedroom. At 11 p.m. I heard a muffled cry. I staggered up the stairs, and just inside the front doorway lay Mrs. Elkmoss, holding the side of her bleeding head and unable to get up.

She had been over at her grandparents that night and, because I had closed the garage door, made a detour over some black ice to get to the front. She slipped, banging her head and left hip. She could not walk and had to crawl to the front door, all the while bleeding profusely from the cut above her eye.

I quickly grabbed a wet washcloth and saw that the laceration above her eye needed stitches. In helping her up, I thought her hip was just bruised and she actually could walk all right. But I also knew there was no help for me. I could see the headlines of the newspaper in the morning. "Thoughtless Husband Tries To Kill Wife," it would read. If the case ever got to trial, I would be found guilty on at least four counts: (1) Going to bed without knowing where my wife was; (2) Closing the garage door, thus locking my wife out of the house; (3) Not hearing the injured whimpers of my wife; and (4) Going to bed too early ("I told him over and over again that 10 p.m. is way too early to go to bed!").

While tending to my stricken wife, I quickly assessed my situation and found it hopeless, even though I thought she would do just fine medically—or should I say flourish. I quickly put her in the car and rushed off to the emergency room where we saw Dr. Hero (as he is now referred to around the Elkmoss house).

Hero immediately sent Mrs. Elkmoss to get x-rays of her hip and finding it okay, expertly sewed up her laceration. Then, surprisingly, he sent her back for x-rays of her wrist. I am positive, in the series of events of stopping her bleeding, helping her to a chair, and later to the ER, she never once said anything about her wrist. But while Hero was fixing her cut, she mumbled something about her wrist and, to quote Mrs. Elkmoss, "That wonderful Dr. Hero immediately looked into the complaint—unlike certain other callous doctors and husbands who will remain nameless!"

When the x-rays came back, all three of us, now at 2 a.m., looked at them. Mrs. Elkmoss and I could not see a thing, but Dr. Hero pointed to a questionable "wrinkle" as he called it, and wondered if it might be a fracture.

The next morning before Hero went home off his night shift, he and I went over the films with the radiologist. Even the radiologist could not make anything out of them.

Meanwhile, Mrs. Elkmoss's wounds healed nicely, except she kept complaining about her wrist. So after about two weeks of listening to her whining, I finally sent her to an orthopedist, Dr. Bones. He was Mrs. Elkmoss's favorite when she worked on the ward. (I think it was because he was handsome, pleasant, competent, and wrote prescriptions such as, "No dishwashing or cleaning windows for a year!")

As you could well predict, x-rays now showed a small non-displaced fracture in her wrist. "See," beamed Mrs. Elkmoss, "Dr. Hero was right again."

The only consolation I could retrieve out of this major disaster to my family reputation (which remains to this day, very poor) is that

Mrs. Elkmoss observed that if she were as old as her grandmother and took a fall on the ice like that, she would have had more than a slightly broken wrist that even her incompetent husband could properly diagnose.

Thus, I have finally detected a small chink in Mrs. Elkmoss's armor of resistance to Southern living. Now, if I can only live to my eighties, I might finally make it to somewhere warm, at least for the winter!

CHAPTER 59
FAMILY MEDICINE

In recent times, there has been a lot of attention on medical errors that could be avoided. For my part (along with the rest of my family), I long ago realized one way to significantly cut down on the number of my medical mistakes is to never treat or advise any friend or family member. There are a lot of reasons why I have traditionally misadvised my family (stupidity being top of the list), but I choose to believe that nothing is really wrong with a loved one. That really clouds my judgment.

Early in our marriage, Mrs. Elkmoss recognized these diagnostic weaknesses in her husband. Probably the most glaring error came when an old friend from residency, Buzzard, came visiting from the South. Buzzard had been a year ahead of me in residency at Southern Fungus Medical University and mentored me. He moved on to Texas his third year and then went into private practice there. We still kept in contact and he was even my best man when I married Mrs. Elkmoss.

After several years of invitations, Buzzard finally agreed to bring his wife and three young kids to visit during the summer and stay during the 4th of July holiday. Although hectic, particularly at the start of the week since the airline lost some of their luggage, the week was a lot of fun. The wives got to do some shopping while husbands watched the kids playing at the lake. There were balloon championships twice a day to see, and even a county fair that the kids particularly enjoyed.

The last day of the visit, I wanted to show Buzzard the hospitals and my office in the morning, then we planned to meet the wives and children at the zoo in the afternoon. We even met some of my colleagues and he was fairly impressed with the practice. On the way to the zoo, however, he started getting a headache. It seemed to start with him not being able to see half a stop sign. By the time we got to the zoo, he was really hurting so I offered to take him to the emergency room.

Buzzard had had trouble with migraine headaches in the past, and he said he just had one as bad as that several weeks earlier. All he wanted to do was to lie down in the back of the car and sleep while everyone else went to the zoo. Even his wife seemed okay with that plan, but not Mrs. Elkmoss. The whole time we were looking a prairie dogs, lions, and monkeys, she was nagging at both Mrs. Buzzard and I to take him to the hospital.

When we got back to the car a couple hours later, Buzzard said he was feeling better and just wanted to go home and sleep it off. The following morning, their plane was leaving early, so we got up only to find Buzzard still with a headache. Mrs. Elkmoss had enough by this time and insisted we take him to the emergency room, but Buzzard was still resistant. Working under the time restraint of getting a five-member family packed and on an airplane in time, Buzzard avoided going to the hospital.

That evening, Mrs. Buzzard called in a panicked voice to report that when they had arrived in Texas that afternoon, Buzzard was still sick. They went to their emergency room to find out he had a cerebral hemorrhage! Thankfully it was small and Buzzard recovered well without ever finding out the cause, but I never did recover from not following the advice of Mrs. Elkmoss.

In truth, I believe I have given my family some very good medical advice over the years, but Mrs. Elkmoss always takes credit for the good suggestions and I get blamed for the bad ones (such as when and when not to get x-rays when kids come home with sore arms and legs from falls). After all, who is ever going to believe recommendations of a neurologist who sent his ailing friend on an airplane ride home with a cerebral hemorrhage?

CHAPTER 60
OLDER SISTERS

There have been several books written about birth order and personalities. I think there is some truth to a few of the theories, but since none of us has a choice in the matter, such discussions seem moot. Take for example Mother Elkmoss. She was the second of three girls. As I was growing up, she talked incessantly about how her older sister got all the praise and her younger sister got all the attention. Sounds like a true middle-child syndrome to me. Maybe that was the reason she had only two children—so there would be no one in the middle.

Two-child syndromes are somewhat different. Sister Elkmoss was born in March, two years before me. I was born in July, so that made her two years *and* four months older. Now, four months might not seem much, but when I was a kid, the fact that Sister Elkmoss could say she was three years older than me for four months a year tended to be irritating.

I probably could have dealt with the age difference better, but I was a scrawny little kid and Sister Elkmoss was huge and tough. She would beat me up and I could not do anything about it except wait until I finally grew big enough to get even. By that time (I think I was eleven or twelve), she claimed she was a girl. Such was the frustration of my childhood as a "little brother."

Some of my frustration was lessened one day when I was about six years old. Our family had been invited to a cottage of some rich friends. They had a pool and even though my sister and I could not swim, we enjoyed floating around in big inner tubes while our parents were having lunch inside. I was goofing around on my tube and slipped through. I floundered and could not grab hold of the tube. To this day, Sister Elkmoss says she does not remember any of this, but for some reason, she floated nearby and was close enough for me to grasp her float, thus saving me. Talk about a grateful little brother!

In our teenage years, sibling order started to generate benefits in my direction. I did not have to fight nearly as hard for allowances or privileges to drive the car. She was a great student and following in her footsteps in school was very easy as well. Sister Elkmoss took all the bumps and bruises of growing up, and I appreciated it.

I always maintain that Sister Elkmoss inherited the brains and beauty in the family, and I was stuck with what was left. That might not be quite right, but there is a lot of evidence over the years to prove my case. No one will deny she is better looking, and she is largely responsible for me getting through my freshman year in college. I was very strong in math and science, but my English skills were sadly lacking. Sister Elkmoss, on the other hand, is very intelligent and had a strong interest in English. For my poetry class, she had learned all the poems I had to study and quizzed me mercilessly the night before my exam so I would be prepared. The general English class was predominantly graded on a huge composition paper. She stayed up the night before it was due, typing and correcting the paper while I slept. Ironically, I, who was majoring in engineering, got "A's" in both poetry and English composition when she, majoring in English, had earned "B's" two years earlier when she took the courses.

There is some further benefit to being a little brother, however. As we get older now, I cannot wait for March to come each year.

Between then and July, I get the opportunity to remind my sister how much older she is than me. As I talk to my young patients now, I always remind them to be kind to their younger siblings because later on, Old Man Time would get even with them.

CHAPTER 61
A NEUROLOGIST'S DOG

Long before I even thought about medical school, let alone specializing in neurology, I was a lieutenant in the Army teaching at a post in the South. The Army also trained dogs on that post, and many of the dogs in the program were Labrador retrievers. If a dog failed, it was sold through property disposal with closed bids. Elkmoss parents did not have a dog at the time, so when I heard about the auction, I put in a low bid thinking they would appreciate a dog. It was unsuccessful, but fortunately a small Lab followed a child of one of the officers in my department home. Since he already had a dog, he let me have the stray.

His kids had named the dog Duchess, but probably the only time I got a diagnosis right about this dog was identifying him as a "Duke" instead. I took the four-month-old puppy home and shortly left for Vietnam. My parents named him Geordie after a favorite story of Father Elkmoss's about Wee Geordie, a ninety-eight-pound weakling type that grew up to be an international strong man.

Unfortunately, Father Elkmoss, the true dog lover in the family, died shortly after I returned from Vietnam. That left Mother Elkmoss with a dog that waged a passive-aggressive battle against her for the next four years while I attended medical school. Mother Elkmoss swore that the dog would wait until she left for work in the morning, and then deliberately lift his leg on the edge of her bed. It is interesting that when I finally took the dog during my internship, I could leave him for more than thirty-six hours at a time and he never once had an accident in my apartment.

Geordie was my constant companion throughout internship, residency, and the first years of private practice and marriage. He was there when the first of three children was born. As our baby became more mobile, he would seek out Geordie and study, with great fascination, the powerful tail. Of course, this would require a few pulls. Not only did Geordie tolerate the assault, he actually seemed to enjoy it, often licking the toddler who giggled in sheer delight. All this horrified Mrs. Elkmoss, a new mother who wanted to protect her baby from every germ in the universe.

Just about this time, my mother-in-law noticed that one side of Geordie's face was getting droopy. I thought it was just from old age, but after several months, even I had to admit that the side of Geordie's noble Labrador head was caving in. One evening, Dr. Blade, a neurosurgeon, and I discussed this case extensively, postulating that Geordie might even have a brain tumor. It finally dawned on us that a dog's face, and particularly his forehead, had much more muscularity than a human's, and that he was just suffering from Bell's palsy, a diagnosis that a third-year medical student could have made. The I-told-you-so look I got from my mother-in-law was the beginning of the downfall of any medical authority I had in the Elkmoss family.

By that time, Geordie was thirteen years old and showing signs of old age. His face was droopy from the Bell's palsy, he had a limp from breaking his front leg a month before I started private practice, and he had additional trouble getting up and down stairs because his hips were deteriorating. Still, he was a happy soul and well loved.

About a year later when I returned home from a trip, Geordie wagged his tail like he always did, but could not get up. Although he did not seem to be in any pain, his hips just did not seem to work right. This called for another consultation with Dr. Blade and we concluded (incorrectly again) that hip dysplasia was the cause of Geordie's problems. I will not tell you where we got some steroids to use (there is such a thing as practicing veterinary medicine without a license), but we tried them and there was no change in our patient. I threw in the towel and took Geordie to see our vet, Dr. Frank.

As I lifted the eighty-pound dog on the table, I explained to Frank that the dog's hip dysplasia was getting worse. Dr. Frank just said, "He's knuckling," seeing that the dog's front and back paws curled as I set him down.

"No," I said, "you don't understand. His back legs aren't working."

"No," Frank said. "He's knuckling."

"Well, I can see that, but he's not getting up because his back legs aren't working right."

Dr. Frank was getting a little impatient with me by that time. He said in a condescending voice, "Dr. Elkmoss, your dog has had a stroke."

If I had chosen a specialty other than neurology, perhaps this bit of news would not have been so decimating. If I had not misdiagnosed the dog's Bell's palsy, my medical credibility might not have been so destroyed. And, if my mother-in-law had not used the same veterinary clinic, I might have been better able to hide my incompetence. But such was not the case. The sadness of putting my beloved dog to sleep was made more poignant with the final knowledge that I had forever lost any confidence that my family had in me as a neurologist.

Even to this day when I attempt to render a medical opinion about our current Labrador, my family members remind me that I am much better off restricting my practice to humans, and "non-family" humans at that.

CHAPTER 62
WINTER DRIVING

I have always been a bad driver on slick roads. I think it is because I had a winter driving by-pass at birth, and whenever there is ice or snow (which is usual for Moss State), I panic. I got a reprieve from the snow during my year internship at Beach Community Hospital, and three more years at Southern Fungus Medical University. When I returned to Moss State, I bought a four-wheel-drive Jeep CJ-7 so I could face the prospect of winter driving with a much more positive attitude. Unlike four-wheel vehicles now, however, when I wanted to switch from two-wheel drive, I had to get out of the Jeep and lock the hubs. Nonetheless, after buying the Jeep in October, I waited patiently for the first snowfall to come so I could zoom around with abandon.

When I woke up Thanksgiving morning, I was greeted with a two-inch snowfall and eagerly ran out to lock the hubs so I could spin around the roads before salt trucks ruined my fun. And I did have lots of fun. For the first time in my life I actually looked forward to snow as opposed to dreading winter.

By January there was lots of snow, but the roads were relatively clear and most of the time I stayed in two-wheel drive. I had started dating the future Mrs. Elkmoss and naturally tried to amaze her with my driving skills. She was not very impressed, maintaining she was a better driver on ice with two-wheel front drive than I would ever be with the CJ-7 in four-wheel drive.

One afternoon, we were driving along on a rural two-lane road when I slid off the road into a snow bank. I got out and trudged through the snow to lock the hubs before trying to get back on the road. Unfortunately, I was too deep in the snow and was not going anywhere.

Just then a fellow with a two-wheel-drive Toyota came by. He got out a towrope, hooked it up, and then whipped us out of the snow bank in less than five minutes. As he collected his towrope, accepted my undying gratitude, and got back in his car, I heard him mumble, "I always wanted to do that!"

When I got back in the Jeep, the future Mrs. Elkmoss did not say anything but she sure did have a smirk on her face. And she has never forgotten the incident, bringing up a slide-by-slide description of the event at many family get-togethers. Every time it snows, she reminds me to be very careful since, even with four-wheel drive, I still do not know how to drive in icy conditions.

Last year on a particularly cold day, she told me to be careful as I left the house. At the end of the block, there is a little hill ending at a "T" in the road with a steep bank on the other side. I, of course, slid right through the intersection and got stuck with my front wheels over the edge. My SUV now has four-wheel drive on the fly, so I whipped it into 4-H only to remain hung up.

I called Mrs. Elkmoss on my cell phone to get the number for AAA service and naturally she had to ask why. After telling her what happened, she asked what she usually does when I do something dumb.

"Should I call my father?"

"No, dear, just give me the tow truck number!"

Thankfully, the tow truck was just minutes away. He got out of his vehicle, took one step on the road, and fell flat on his back. As I helped him up, he said, "Wow, it sure is slick out here!"

He had my car back on the road and I was off to work after just a total of twenty minutes from sliding off the road. Every family get-together when the subject of my driving abilities is brought up, I quickly point out how even the tow truck driver fell. I do not think it does anything for my reputation, but it at least makes me feel a little better.

CHAPTER 63
DIETS

When Dr. Richard Atkins, proponent of the famous low-carbohydrate diet, almost died when he went into a cardiac arrhythmia, he was quick to point out that his heart problems had nothing to do with his diet. For many years, the nutrition community had been having a fit trying to prove his diet was harmful, so they had a ball with poor (or should I say rich?) Dr. Atkins's malady.

I have been on many diets (some with a little semblance of reasonableness) since undergraduate school, so while the controversy continues surrounding the Atkins Diet, let me share with you some "truths" I have learned.

When graduating from high school, I weighted approximately 175 pounds and was probably as healthy as I could be. Four years later after undergraduate school, I weighed 230 pounds. Now I know the obvious conclusion is that one should avoid college, but that is not my point. One might also think that the Army would try to avoid using a 230-pound toad, but this was in the Vietnam era, and I was drafted. After Basic Training, Advanced Individual Training, Officer Candidate School, and about three and a half million push-ups, I weighed 180 pounds, could run with sixty-five pounds of field gear on my back all day (and night sometimes), and still eat double rations without gaining weight.

After a year Stateside and fattening up again, I was sent to Vietnam. Before they found me in Saigon and sent me near the DMZ for the rest of the year, I had a taste of local food and learned a valuable lesson: never eat pizza in a Far East country.

In the Continental Hotel across the street from the Palace in Saigon, I ordered the only thing I could recognize—pizza. It did look like pizza, but you would have to take a cheap frozen one, over cook it, and then spread dirty grass on it to look like the one I was served. Yuk!

I survived Vietnam, but not by eating local food. Coming back from Vietnam, then, I weighed 175 pounds and was again, in the best of health. It leads me to my First Truth: I'd rather be fat than fight.

I started medical school then, and in several years my weight started creeping up again. It was about that time that the original Atkins Diet came out and I jumped on the program as only a dumb medical student who should know better could. The Atkins Diet called for avoiding carbohydrates and putting myself into ketosis that I checked by dip-sticking my urine. I suspect that the biggest problem Atkins had in selling his program was to convince people that messing around with their own excrements is in any way tolerable.

The medical school apartments where I stayed were conveniently located across the street from a major grocery store. Convenient is a great term because it was at that time OPEC tightened the supply of oil. Gasoline became scarce and the lines at service stations became interminable. It was of great benefit to have a grocery store across the street from where I stayed.

One day while looking for Atkins-approved food at the grocery store, I came across a sale on T-bone steaks. For a dollar apiece, I could buy a twelve-ounce steak. There were thirty steaks in the freezer and I had $30 in my pocket, so I bought them all.

For the next month, then, I only ate eggs for breakfast and steaks for dinner. The morning after eating the final steak (It amazes me that I still like eating steaks today), I weighed myself. Much to my amazement, I had actually gained four pounds! This leads me to my Second Truth: I can gain weight on any diet.

The final truth about diets that I would like to share came to me years later after getting married and gaining forty pounds of blubber. I finally got tired of Mrs. Elkmoss telling me to "suck it in" when standing up and I already had exhaled as much as possible and was hypoxic. A TV commercial at the time (just after a plug for juicy burgers) advertised a national diet chain, Fat Boys Unlimited, which had just opened an office in Swampville.

I called the place and signed up for the program. It involved buying a week's worth of their food (ten times the cost of a month of steaks in medical school), keeping a log, and returning the following week for an official weigh-in. I listened not so carefully to the instructions and went about my business that first week. To be truthful, the food I had purchased was so bland I felt I needed to supplement it a little. I failed to record the "supplements" on my log sheet, feeling that if it was not recorded, it did not exist.

The following week when I weighed in, I had actually gained two pounds on their diet. My diet counselor looked up and had the audacity to accuse me of cheating. When I raised the possibility that I just might be one of those people whose metabolism was slow (after all, I had already proved, in Truth #2 above, that I could gain weight on any diet), she promptly pulled out a study from the *New England Journal of Medicine* that carefully looked into that question. The article reported on thirty people monitored on a big diet program. They found that for the thirteen people who had gained weight, all had under-reported their intakes. In other words, my indignant counselor said, absolutely everyone who did not lose weight, lied!

I got the message, bought another week's worth of expensive food, and went home with my tail between my fat legs. I faithfully followed the diet and amazingly lost nearly ten pounds by the following week. With that success, I was hooked and became a diet zealot. I also realized that the diet center was ripping people off with the exorbitant prices charged for their foods. After all, Weight-Watchers had practically the same diet, and you are supposed to prepare the food yourself. The following week, I explained to my counselor that I had enough food left over from the two weeks before. Since she was the one who caught me lying on my food log initially, she believed me. The next couple of weeks she was on vacation or something, and the new counselors (by that time I was being passed around from one to another) thought I had bought enough the previous weeks. The result was that I was losing weight fast and it was not costing me anything.

You would think that Mrs. Elkmoss would have been extremely happy about the situation, but she was not. The more weight I lost and the less it cost, the more concerned she was that something was wrong. She started to think I was losing too much weight, and I looked too sickly. Paradoxically, she pointed out that I was not exercising properly. I played video games while sitting on the exercise bike, and in the heat of the game I slowed down too much. She felt that was not exercise. (My argument to her was that if my rear end was on an exercise bike and I had exercise clothes on, I was EXERCISING regardless of what my feet were doing.)

In the middle of this successful program, the diet center went bankrupt. I used to tell everyone that it was because I refused to buy their food, but I think it was about the same time McDonald's found, with the failure of their McLean Deluxe, that American people just do not want to be skinny. (Well, maybe they want to be skinny; they just do not want to give up their fat food.) A year later when I started to gain some weight back, Mrs. Elkmoss changed from griping about me being too skinny to yelling about me eating too much. I came to understand the final truth. When I was fat, she nagged. When I was losing weight, she nagged. When I was skinny, she nagged. When I was my ideal weight and as good as I could be physically, she nagged. I am now fat again, and she is still nagging. The Final Truth (and most important): Nagging has nothing to do with my weight!

CHAPTER 64
TITLE IX

It has been many years since Title IX, which attempted to bring equality between males and females in sports, was enacted. Equality is a very difficult term to apply here because my medical textbooks still maintain that men and women have distinct differences in physical make-up. But as I look back, I remember learning about gender equality in sports long before some federal legislation said I had to.

I was introduced to the game of tennis the summer after my eighth-grade year. By the following summer, I thought I was "great stuff." After all, I had beaten all my school buddies (I was careful to pick only those who wore glasses or whose birth-name was Klutz) and had even taken on some upperclassmen successfully. At that point in my budding tennis career, I decided that I only wanted to play people who were better than me. Consequently, I would never play with girls.

Towards the end of the summer, I had the opportunity to attend a month-long speech institute where other rising tenth-graders from all over the state stayed on Moss State University campus and learned about theater, oral interpretation, and debate. It was a great experience taking all of the "hey y'all's" and "young'ns" out of our vocabularies. There was only one draw back—not enough tennis. The only time we could play was a designated free time between 3 and 5 p.m. in the afternoon. Not only that, I did not know anyone, let alone tennis players, and all I could do was hit the ball against the training wall near the courts.

One day early in the camp, I noticed someone also hitting the ball against one of the walls. After much observation and study, I determined that the player was a female. I was desperate for someone to play, so I violated my fundamental rule about playing against a girl.

Her name was Missy (those days every young lady in sports was nicknamed Missy), and as I recall, I only scored one point in the three sets we played! She was very polite and thanked me for playing and went on back to the dorm. Later I found out she represented Moss State that year in the National Junior Chamber of Commerce Tennis Championships and had won the title for her age bracket.

You would think I had learned my lesson, and I really had, but after graduating from high school and starting college, I slipped up again. One could argue that drinking is not a sport, but Moss State University was listed as one of the top party schools in the country, and the students considered drinking a varsity event. I pledged a fraternity my freshman year, and in trying to make myself look good, made a passing comment about there not being a girl in the university who could out-drink me. (The lawmakers back then let us drink beer and wine at eighteen.)

That was like running a beanie up the fraternity flagpole. So my "brothers-to-be" promptly fixed me up with a date who resembled Helga from the WWF for a big fraternity party that weekend. Fortunately, she was living in a dorm a block away from the frat house, so transportation was not a problem. (I do not think a bus could have fit her in.) My only sports jacket was freshly dry-cleaned and I was ready to party…

As best I remember, I did not last an hour with this "lady." By nine o'clock, I wandered up to an empty room upstairs in the fraternity house and lay down. She was still going strong when a group of laughing brothers woke me up to remind me I had only fifteen minutes to get her back to the dorm before the midnight curfew. She was giggling and carrying on by the time we got to the dorm steps. I leaned over to give her a kiss (so I could return to the frat house with my tie tossed over my shoulder—indicating I had received a kiss). She got sick and threw up on me. Not only did I return to the fraternity in disgrace of having been out drunk by a girl, I had ruined my only sports jacket and almost got kissed by the Greek goddess of eating.

During the depressive stupor of the next several weeks, I tried to figure out how to repair the damage to my male ego. It came to me while sitting in a large, very hard chemistry class, taught by a tough German professor ("Zhere is no voom vor stupidity, Mr. Elkzmozz!"). Sitting just in front of me was Candy, the sister of the most famous basketball player in the history of Moss State. While I could not personally claim superiority over women in any sport, I thought if I could just get a date with Candy, I might regain some meager standing in the male community.

And getting a date with Candy was not really that hard. Even though she was fairly good-looking and came with the impressive credentials of having a famous brother, she had a couple of characteristics that tended to keep fellows away from her. First, she was tall. But I was taller, so that did not bother me. Then too, she was brilliant. I was struggling a little with chemistry, so that actually could be a benefit. Finally, though, she was mean and nasty. I was in a state of desperation by then, so I rationalized that it would be for just one date, enough to rescue my reputation.

Wonders of wonders...she accepted my invitation. There was a dance held at the old student center, and I parked near a ten-foot bank leading down to a small stream.

I had retrieved my puked-on sports coat from the cleaners, and thought I was looking pretty good. The dance was well-attended (which is why I had to park on the road), and both my date and I started having a good time.

Later in the evening, the dance floor really was quite crowded. Candy and I were laughing and dancing when we bumped into a really big guy, every bit of six feet, eight inches tall. I said, "Excuse me," but Candy said, "Watch it, buddy!" The big guy kind of grunted and danced away from us.

A little later, we bumped into him again and Candy cussed as I whisked her away quickly. I was not fast enough the third time, however. When we bumped him, Candy grabbed the big lug, spun him around, and yelled, "Hit him, Herman. Hit him!"

It was all I could do to get her to let go of the giant. I insisted that we had to go home right away, and Candy finally acquiesced. She was still discussing how she would have knocked his block off with a combination punch to his "belt area" when we got to her side of the car parked on the edge of the bank. Just as I unlocked the door she swung around, I think trying to demonstrate some boxing technique, and we both went tumbling down the embankment into the small stream. I ended up face down in the stream with Candy lying on my head, and I could not move her. I distinctly remember thinking how it would be ironic that I drown in four inches of water, trying to regain some sort of superiority over the female gender. Luckily, she finally let me up and I could get a breath.

The next day, when I returned the muddy sports coat to the cleaners, I briefly reflected that it might have been more merciful to drown than face the humiliation of explaining how a girl had messed up my best outfit again.

A few years after that, Congress passed Title IX, and I never said a word. I was too scared Helga would come and find me. It is only now, more than thirty years later, that I have recovered enough courage to comment on gender equality in sports.

CHAPTER 65
TENNESSEE FISHERMEN

One of my bigger shortcomings in life has been the inability to fish. It is not only that I cannot get into the rhythm of jigging or some other manner of casting, but even after spending hundreds of hours learning how to tie surgical knots in medical school, I have not been able to securely tie hooks on fishing lines. To make matters worse, or perhaps because of my inadequacies, I cannot seem to generate any interest in sitting out in a boat all day demonstrating my incompetence. I will not even begin to discuss my aversion to ice fishing.

Early in our marriage, Mrs. Elkmoss did not really care that I had little interest in fishing. In fact, I even overheard her bragging to friends one day that she would never let her husband go out fishing for a week with a bunch of other men. All that changed when the three Elkmoss children came along, especially the two oldest who were boys. The pressure for me to fish really became intense when we moved to a house on a lake. The nagging to take the boys, four and six years old, fishing was comparable to her trying to teach three males of the house to raise (or is it lower?) the toilet seat.

I do not know about other fathers of young boys, but I was panicky with the thought of two hooligans whipping around fishing poles with sharp hooks on the ends. I would think the safest creatures in that scenario would be the fish. The person most in danger would be me.

It was then that I hit upon an idea. I took two excited boys down to the lake and out on the water in our boat. I then tied somewhat rubbery worm-looking lures, without hooks, on the end of their lines with sinkers and let them fish for hours. I brought along a book and got some wonderful reading time. The boys were tickled to death to splash their Mickey Mouse fishing gear around, and Mrs. Elkmoss felt like she had successfully nagged her husband. I finished out that season and was well into the next season when my fishing world came crashing down around me.

After practicing medicine in Tennessee, completing his neurology residency several years after I did, and then spending a couple years private practice, my old medical school buddy, Kildeer, joined my other partner and me.

Every spring, Kildeer's Tennessee buddies, about ten or so, would spend a week fishing in Canada. He went the first year after he had joined our practice and had such a good time that he asked his father and me to come the following year. Mrs. Elkmoss actually encouraged me to go because she wanted us to take her grandfather, Gump, who was a great fishing enthusiast. That way, Father Kildeer would have some company his own age.

The fishing camp was set up so that we stayed in four-man cabins. We all ate breakfast in the lodge every morning, then picked up our gear and lunch stuff, got into small boats that could hold two men and a guide (for every two boats), and went fishing for the day. At noon, the guide would cook a shore lunch with the fish we caught.

On the third day, our two boats with one guide went with five other boats, the ten Tennessee boys and another guide to a remote huge finger lake. We spent the morning traveling all the way to the end of the lake and caught only two small pike, hardly enough to feed the bunch of us for lunch. By 1 p.m. we were getting pretty hungry, so the two guides, Native Americans, suggested we start trolling. Gump and I, along with our guide, took off with Kildeer and his father behind, while the rest of the Tennessee crowd went off with the other guide on the other side of lake.

After a half-hour or so of slow trolling and no nibbles, I was falling asleep. The guide looked back and could not see the other boat. We turned around, and on our way back we finally saw the Kildeers on the other side of the lake. Kildeer was in the bow motioning frantically. As we got closer, we could see Father Kildeer sitting in the middle of the boat, jumping around. When we got alongside, we saw an enormous fish weighing more than twenty-seven pounds. Unfortunately, it was a big Muskie that was out of season. Kildeer took it around to all his Tennessee friends. The more he showed it, the hungrier we all got. Finally, someone suggested we eat it, but Kildeer wanted to keep it and have it mounted. After the guides convinced him he would be imprisoned if caught with the Muskie out of season, he consented. It was the only time I ever ate Muskie and it was delicious. Hard to tell if it tasted so good because of the way it was cooked or just because it was illegal.

The next morning as we were sitting around the dining room table eating breakfast and reminiscing about the Muskie, the conversation turned to living on the lake. One thing led to another and I started bragging about how I fished with my children without any hooks. There was a noticeable silence and you see the Tennessee boys literally scooting their chairs away from me. For the rest of the week, those good old boys had nothing to do with me.

Gump noticed all that and when we got back and before he left for his home, he took his two great-grandsons down to the lake and promptly taught them how to fish with hooks. They all returned with a bucket of some twenty-five to thirty very small sunfish. Gump proceeded to fillet them, getting less than a bite from each side of the fish. All that was fine with me, but the day after Gump left, the boys sneaked down to the lake and brought back another bucket of fish. Mrs. Elkmoss then made me clean them all. I am lucky to have all my fingers!

My difficulties with fishing continue today. I still cannot tie a lure correctly, but if I ever do catch another fish, at least I will know how to filet the darn thing.

CHAPTER 66
THE YUCCA PLANT

Mrs. Elkmoss and I have had a very long-running disagreement about plants. She is of the opinion that natural flowers and green things should be kept in the house. I, on the other hand, feel that I have spent thousands of dollars for a house to keep Mother Nature out. In my opinion, the only good houseplant is a dead one. When I look around our home, however, I am convinced that both mothers, Elkmoss and Nature, are winning the battle.

Maybe my aversion to nature goes back to childhood when I dreaded having to mow the extensive lawn around the old Elkmoss estate. Whatever the reason, I just did not want growing things in my house until my experience with a yucca plant.

After having our first child, Mrs. Elkmoss and I decided to move. The house we found was just a couple of blocks away and was owned by an alcoholic lady, Delores. When Drunk Delores moved out that summer, she left two items that she dearly loved—a cat and a yucca plant. The cat apparently had been missing when she left, and the yucca plant had been too big to move off the back porch. We knew Drunk Delores really wanted her cat and yucca plant because months and even a year later she would ring our doorbell, inebriated and crying, and ask if we had seen a gray cat or if she could see her plant. We always told her no; we had destroyed the yucca plant and had not seen her cat. But, of course, we were nurturing her plant and had seen her cat wandering around the house fairly often.

Every summer, Delores had moved the plant out the back door to flourish in Moss State's sunshine (such that it is). In the winter she would move it to the bottom of the steps in the house where it could grow as high as two stories, protected from winter weather. It was about ten feet high when we first inherited the plant. We continued the practice of moving the plant twice a year by having a family get-together scheduled every fall and spring so the men folk could move the plant in or out depending on the season. One year, the bottom of the old half-barrel holding the plant fell apart, making a big mess. Luckily there was a sale on old barrels at our friendly hardware store, and we saved the plant.

As the years went by, it grew and I developed a deep attachment to the yucca plant. When it became a fifteen-foot monster, and particularly after the barrel fell apart, Mrs. Elkmoss wanted to get rid of it. Now that was a switch. There I was, the greatest nature-hater of all time, pleading for the life of plant while one of the biggest tree-huggers in the world was advocating its demise.

The somewhat extended argument was settled during a long weekend when I was away at a conference. In what I have labeled "The Great Chainsaw Massacre," Mrs. Elkmoss cut up the yucca plant and threw it away. Well, not all away. My mother-in-law, bless her heart, apparently saved a piece of the plant and it is now living at her house. (I am not completely sure I believe that, but I give my mother-in-law great credit for soothing my hurt feelings.) I was a shattered yucca lover, and I am not sure I will ever recover from my anguish. To this day, whenever Mrs. Elkmoss wants to bring in another plant from the great outdoors, I keep telling her, "Remember the yucca plant!"

As part of therapy to recover from my great loss, maybe I should buy a stuffed cat at Goodwill, save a bunch of wood chips, and keep them in a paper bag in the entryway closet. If Drunk Delores ever shows up at my door again looking for her missing animal and plant, I could hand her the bag and say, "Here's your damn cat and yucca plant!" On the other hand, that would preclude me from enlisting the aid of PETA or the Sierra Club. So I just will go on chanting my mantra, "Remember the yucca plant!"

CHAPTER 67
HIP REPLACEMENT

There comes a point after a dog joins a family that it no longer is a pet, but a full-fledged member of the pack. (Any dog owner knows that families are instantly reorganized into a pack when they adopt a dog.) Usually that happens on the way back from acquiring the animal, but I think in the latest case, it occurred when our youngest child first laid eyes on a black Labrador retriever, later named Coal.

The wife of an orthopedic surgeon, Harry Cole, called Mrs. Elkmoss the day after our old dog had died. She expressed sympathy for the Elkmosses and explained that their male registered dog had gotten loose and had mated with another pedigree Lab down the street. That dog had a litter of puppies (out of wedlock, of course). The Coles were suitably embarrassed and had no interest in the pick of the litter to which they were entitled. They kindly offered the distressed Elkmoss family their choice.

It turned out that the dog chose us when he jumped on the littlest Elkmoss child. At home, the first order of business was to name the new family member, and it did not take Mrs. Elkmoss very long. She named him Coal. I even thought it was quite clever.

About a year later I was attending an advisory meeting with Dr. Cole's partner, Bones, and a nice psychologist, Sigmund, who worked with many of our patients. I explained what a nice dog Dr. Cole had given us and bragged how clever my wife was in coming up with his name. Bones piped up that he and Sigmund had brothers from another litter. Bones said that his dog was also named Coal, and Sigmund, from the other side of the table said, "Yeah, and my dog's name is Harry!"

I later ran into Dr. Cole and pointed out that there sure were a lot of dogs named after him. That reminded him of a story about a renowned obstetrician who was the head of a large residency program. The program staffed many free clinics in their city and the residents delivered a great number of babies for the community. Often times, the new mother would ask the resident who delivered their baby for a suggestion of a name. At first, the young physicians would recommend the name of their famous attending out of respect. As the custom became more popular and with a feminized conversion used for baby girls, literally hundreds of infants were named for this professor. When the residency chief finally found out what was going on, he hit the roof and told his staff that he was going to check all birth certificates issued in the area from then on. If his name ever appeared again, he would personally castrate the resident who delivered the baby—without anesthesia! In the same sense, Harry Cole told us that he would appreciate it if no more dogs were named after him. As far as I know, he got his wish.

Coal really was a terrific dog, but as he got older, his hips started to deteriorate. On a routine checkup one year for heartworms, I made the mistake of letting Mrs. Elkmoss take the dog in to our beloved veterinarian, Dr. Frank. We were not the only ones that thought highly of this vet. For years he participated in a Saturday morning call-in show for the local radio station, so almost everyone knew and liked him. When asked about the hips, he quickly took some x-rays and announced that Coal had hip dysplasia. One of the options was to take the dog to Moss State University Veterinary School and have his hips replaced.

For months our family dinners were filled with discussions about getting the dog's hips fixed. I seemed to be the only one with sense enough to realize that you do not subject a free dog that was seventy-seven years old in human years to a $6,000 procedure.

One Saturday as I was driving home from making rounds at the hospital, I turned on the radio and almost wrecked the car when I heard a voice that sounded like Mrs. Elkmoss asking Dr. Frank about hip dysplasia. He explained the disease and what was involved with hip replacement surgery.

Mrs. Elkmoss asked, "What should I tell my husband who thinks it is ridiculous to spend so much money fixing the dog's hips?"

Dr. Frank quickly said, "Oh, just tell him to go buy a lottery ticket!"

By the time I got home, the radio show was over. As I walked in the door, the telephone was ringing and Mrs. Elkmoss answered it. It was Dr. Cole (also a faithful listener to Dr. Frank on Saturday mornings) who had recognized Mrs. Elkmoss's voice.

"You tell that husband of yours that I always thought he was a cheap bastard!"

I withstood the enormous pressure to subject our beloved dog to major surgery. For his part, Coal hobbled around, a fairly happy soul, oblivious to the dynamics of the situation. Unfortunately, he developed bone cancer six months later and we finally had to put him to sleep. My feeling of vindication was permanently erased by the looks I received when I pointed out that at least his last year of life was not marred by having to go through horrendous hip replacement surgery.

Over the years and with experiences of having several dogs as pets, I have come to realize that I would be the first one to be placed in a dog house—long before any animal in the Elkmoss house. So I have learned to sit quietly as dog after dog is permitted to get up on furniture and even, heaven sakes, sleep in our bed. Recently, I have started to develop a little hip pain myself. When I mentioned it to Mrs. Elkmoss, she said, "Just live with it. Remember what you said about Coal and his hips!"

CHAPTER 68
SHORT

When I was growing up, I was almost always taller than other kids my age and easily took my height for granted. I never thought of size as being an issue except when studying someone like Napoleon. There was one exception, however. In my fourth year of medical school and rotating in surgery at a VA hospital in the South, the chief resident was a tall but very mild and pleasant fellow (quite unusual for a surgeon, I might add). He was a good eight inches taller than me at six feet, three inches, and I felt very intimidated around him. When looking in at various surgery procedures, I could usually just stand behind folks anywhere at the table but even to scrub in with this gentle behemoth, I had to stand on two stepstools. The poor short scrub nurses had to use as many as seven or eight stools. The surgery scene looked like a miniature castle with surgical assistants standing on the turrets and the chief resident lording over the place. I do not think he got very many surgeries with the attendings because they would refuse to accommodate him by having to stand on stepstools themselves.

For the most part, however, I have been very comfortable being tall and rarely had to think about being short—that is, short in the sense of height. There are lots of other ways to be short, however. After finishing a complicated financial planning review, the advisor started using the word "short" to describe my predicament. That got me thinking (always a dangerous condition), and I realized that I had really been financially "short" all my life.

I first became financially short in high school. It corresponded with getting a driver's license, dating, and an allowance. My parents gave me $2 a week and, coincidentally, I seemed to always be $2 short. Sister Elkmoss was a "saver," and not only saved money, but would save my dating life by loaning me some money.

Times moved on along with inflation. When I went to college, my allowance increased to $50 a month, and, wonders of wonders, I seemed to be about $50 short every month. As a popular country western song at the time said, "There was too much month left at the end of my money."

I did get somewhat of a reprieve from my shortness for the three years I was in the service. For the first year, I was in basic and advanced individual training and then officer candidate school, so I did not have any way to spend money. The last year I was in Vietnam and I only had to spend money for beer. At a nickel a can, even the most ardent drunk could not spend much money. For the year before going overseas, I regained my appreciation for being short. After OCS, another candidate and I spent a week's leave in Puerto Rico. It cost me $200. For the rest of the year, I tried to save $200 for a boat trailer for a sailboat. I also seemed to always be a week short of leave time to do the things I wanted to do!

After the service, I got into medical school. Although the GI bill helped, I still seemed to always be that same $200 short each month. I made it through with parental help and then moved on to internship. There, I continued to be $200 short every month. That correlated with the cost of a motorcycle and gear I bought from Kildeer.

During my three years of residency, I was always $2,000 short. I am not sure, but it might have corresponded to a replacement for the motorcycle. By the time I started private practice, I needed to borrow $2,000 from Mother Elkmoss to buy a new house. Finally, however, I was making adequate money and seemed to be on Easy Street. When I got married, both Mrs. Elkmoss and I were working, so it looked like I had permanently corrected my "shortness." Then came the first baby followed by a new house and a whole host of complicating factors. As middle age approached, this led to more serious financial planning, and hence, the latest assessment.

The bottom line is, with my children's college expenses, housing, and all the other costs involved with retirement, I am $2 million short. When I came home and Mrs. Elkmoss, who is fairly tall herself, asked me how it went with the advisor, I told her we were short $2 million. Trying to be funny, she said, "How can such a tall person like you be so short?"

I did not laugh.

CHAPTER 69

DEER TEETH

I have always believed that parents should be closely involved in the education of their children. After raising three children, however, Mrs. Elkmoss and I continue to argue as to what is too involved and becomes pathologic enabling. And in our family, the pathology is usually directed towards me. When I think enough help is enough help, the Elkmoss children run to their mother. Then I get charged and convicted of bad parenting. It has happened enough in the past that you will never see me nominated for Father-of-the-Year Award.

Philosophical considerations of parenting notwithstanding, the alarms went off one Sunday evening just after the start of a high school semester in science for our teenage daughter. Mrs. Elkmoss dutifully asked Kid Elkmoss how her homework was going and was told about a project in class that they were starting the next day. One of the mothers of their group was a dental hygienist and had offered to provide teeth so the students could brush with various toothpastes and measure the amount of erosion. I am sure the kids thought this might provide useful data to get out of brushing their teeth.

At the last minute, the hygienist decided she did not have time or perhaps thought it would enable her child too much to provide the needed teeth for the project. In a mad conference with the other kids in the group, they decided that small, cut pieces of bone would work as well. So at 10 p.m. on a Sunday night, Mrs. Elkmoss (after all, she could not let her only daughter out at night to shop) was wheeling a shopping cart around the supermarket trying to find ten different brands of toothpaste (with and without whiteners) and some bones. The only ones she could find were long beef femurs packaged for sale as dog bones.

At the checkout line, Mrs. Elkmoss tried to explain that she was not emulating a serial killer by storing body parts in her refrigerator, but the clerk did not pay any attention.

Next, Mrs. Elkmoss tried to get tendons and marrow from the bones. She solved that problem by meticulously boiling (now at 1 a.m.) the femurs, then cutting and pulling out the stubborn tissues. I was sound asleep by that time, only to be wakened at 5 a.m. and told to saw the bones into little pieces. I dutifully took the first piece out to the garage and tried to cut it with a saber saw. CLUNK. I hardly scratched the surface of the bone.

When this major setback was explained to the Elkmoss Kid (who got a regular night's rest, mind you), she thought it would probably be okay if she turned in the bones by Wednesday. Then Mrs. Elkmoss called her father (which she always does when she thinks her husband is incompetent). He had lots of tools and she thought I could take the bones over to his house later that day to see if we could cut them up.

Mid-morning, I called a good friend and an oral surgeon, Dr. Payne, and explained the problem. Payne told me that I would need a butcher's saw to cut bones (which I already knew). He also said that if I had called the week before, I could have had more than a hundred teeth, but he had thrown them out. He thought he could collect a hundred more in two weeks and promised to start collecting them. I thought I had done my good deed for the day, but when I told Mrs. Elkmoss the good news, she had a fit. It would be too long; Kid Elkmoss needed the teeth right away.

One of the girls in the office overheard the conversation and pointed out that deer season had just started and I might get the needed teeth from a meat processor. I immediately called the first one listed in the telephone book. When I told him about the science project, he put me on hold to go ask his boss. He came back on the line and said, "Sure, we have all the deer heads you want, but you'll have to pull the teeth yourself."

"Well," I said, trying to figure out how many plastic bags I needed to bring to carry the heads home, "how many teeth do deer have?"

"I don't know," the fellow replied. "I tried to look into one of the heads to count and it bit me!"

When I picked up the deer heads, the boss was there and told me deer typically had thirty-three teeth (which I thought was an odd number for anyone, let alone Bambi), so I grabbed five deer head and came home to ponder the problem of how to pull 165 deer teeth, more than enough to account for breakage, etc. It was difficult just to open the mouths of the poor deer, let alone extract teeth. I tried plain pliers, then vise grips, and finally returned to the pliers again. By the time I was finished there were loose jaws, broken teeth, and grotesque looking deer heads lying around the garage. There I was, holding a utility knife in one hand and a set of pliers in the other. If the police had driven by and looked into the garage at that time (it took more than three hours), they would have surely arrested me. When they found the leftover femurs Mrs. Elkmoss had in the refrigerator, they would have been totally convinced they had caught a mass murderer. Even after I cleaned up the body parts and safely put them in plastic bags, I still had a problem of figuring out what to do with five mangled deer heads (without getting cited for pollution). Luckily, just as I finished putting the last deer head in a bag, Mrs. Elkmoss drove up and told me to quickly put the bags in the garbage bin out on the street since she had just passed the garbage truck. We peered out behind the window shades as the trash people dumped our garbage into the cavernous truck, never once seeing the mayhem I had generated.

I could only get about seventy teeth that were anywhere reasonable to brush, but after Mrs. Elkmoss boiled them for the twentieth time (It was okay that her husband got mad cow disease, scrapie, or whatever deer get, but not her child!), Kid Elkmoss announced that they would do.

Two weeks later after the science project was safely launched and the students were brushing away on the deer teeth, Dr. Payne called to proudly announce he had collected more than 100 teeth for the project. I did not have the heart (or stomach for that matter) to tell him what I had done, so I just gratefully picked up the jar of teeth and set it on the workbench (the same place I had mangled the five deer heads). That disgusted Mrs. Elkmoss, and she finally threw them away.

I never did see the final report about toothpaste and deer teeth, but Kid Elkmoss thought the study was showing that the more you brush your teeth, the heavier they became. I concluded that the more involved I get in a kid's science project, the more insane I become.

CHAPTER 70
GAS LEAKS

Mrs. Elkmoss is a dedicated housekeeper, and to this day I still catch her running a vacuum just before the maid comes ("I don't want the maid to think we have a dirty house!"). Such demands on the sweeper put a lot of wear and tear on the machine and her vacuum cleaners frequently fall apart.

Early in our marriage as a Christmas present, I thought a super deluxe industrial strength vacuum cleaner would be ideal gift—WRONG!! Mrs. Elkmoss pouted for several days, and still on Christmas Eve when our extended family gets together to open presents, the story is told of my gross callousness. She continues to over-use vacuum cleaners, but I am not permitted to buy her one.

Another rule I learned early was never criticize my bride's cooking. I would like to point out that I got my insensitivity about cooking from Father Elkmoss. He was a good, kind soul with a heart of gold, but he never talked much, let alone spontaneously complimented Mother Elkmoss on her rather exceptional cooking abilities. Family stories have it that in response to a question about whether he liked a particularly good dinner that Mother Elkmoss had spent hours preparing, he just said, "I ate it, didn't I?" How can one expect a son of a man like that to be very smart about complimenting his new wife about her less-than-exceptional (and I am choosing these words carefully) cooking abilities?

Although Mrs. Elkmoss is not particularly good at cooking many different foods like Mother Elkmoss, what dishes she does prepare, she does well. One such dish is meatloaf. On an early occasion I mistakenly raised the issue about whether it might be a little redundant to have it three nights in a row, but I quickly learned to say, "Oh, boy, meatloaf!"

Besides cleaning the house and cooking several dishes well, Mrs. Elkmoss has an excellent nose for smells. She got that trait from her mother, and both together could probably out-track a pack of hounds on a fox trail. One day, Mrs. Elkmoss smelled something funny in the family room downstairs in our ranch-type house. My sniffer is terrible, but I did not know it at the time. I smelled nothing, so Mrs. Elkmoss asked her mother to come over to settle the argument. My mother-in-law is perhaps even more conscientious than her daughter (which is hard to believe), and after dutifully sniffing around the house, concluded there must be a gas leak. I am not quite as dumb as I act, so I quickly called the gas company. They sent someone right away, even before my mother-in-law left, and he found a small leak in a gas line to the fireplace. Mrs. Elkmoss was vindicated, my mother-in-law felt she had saved the lives of her child, son-in-law, and future grandchildren, and I was left feeling like a non-smelling jerk!

Several months after that, I came home after a rather tiresome day to be greeted by the strong smell of meatloaf cooking in the oven.

"Oh, boy, meatloaf!"

We sat down and really did have a good dinner. There was some of the excellent meatloaf left over and Mrs. Elkmoss packed it up for sandwiches. (Oh, boy, meatloaf sandwiches!)

Later that evening, Mrs. Elkmoss came up from the family room and while traveling through the dinette, smelled something funny. She called me out of deep thought somewhere. By then I knew enough not to question her nose. To tell the truth, I also smelled something this time. We went downstairs to the fireplace, but that did not seem to be where the smell was coming from. After sniffing around like a beagle after a scent and finding nothing, Mrs. Elkmoss called her mother. She was over more quickly than I thought possible, hoping to add another great save to her credit.

Mother-in-Law also smelled something funny when she came into the dinette off the kitchen, but could not really say what it was. She raised the question of it being gas. Not wanting to have egg on my face again, I promptly called the gas company.

It was the same man who months earlier found the gas leak in the fireplace, but this time he could not detect a problem. We then went upstairs and outside beside the dinette to the gas meter. There, he used an even more sophisticated electronic sniffer that he stuck in the ground around the gas pipe. There was no leak. We went to the dinette and then retraced the gas line in the house as much as possible. Still no leak.

Then in a flash of brilliance, I took the gasman to the refrigerator. I pulled out the meatloaf and unwrapped it. When the sniffer came near my dinner, it beeped, scaring both of us.

I thanked the gasman quietly and made it a point not to tell Mrs. Elkmoss about our discovery. A little later I explained to Mrs. Elkmoss that it was just some strange smell that should be gone by the next morning.

Several years later I did give Mrs. Elkmoss a Christmas present of a book entitled, *1001 Ways to Cook Meatloaf*. She did not think that was too bad of a present, certainly not in the league of a vacuum cleaner!

CHAPTER 71
HAIRCUTS

Kildeer and I have been carefully putting together a book about Moss State wives so that future out-of-state husbands will have some sort of guidance to avoid major *faux pas* in marriage. One of the earliest chapters will be the observation that Moss State women are always terribly distressed when they get a haircut. No matter how carefully the hair stylist tends to Mrs. Elkmoss' hair, she always comes home distraught.

I also have a genetic defect that no book on Moss State women will help. Unlike my middle child, I almost never notice even the most major of hairdo changes. Therefore, haircuts around our house are major events, and I have grown to expect problems. With that in mind, I would like to report on a very unusual and unexpected incident.

One morning, I started making rounds in the Intensive Care Unit and saw a young high school student. He had had a major seizure the night before and was intubated to protect his airway while so obtunded. Fortunately, his seizures stopped and he was waking up. When I saw him, he could open his eyes on command, but he was not with it enough to hold up fingers on command. Later that afternoon I went to my favorite barber, a "man's barber" that my Moss State wife abhors, and received a long overdue haircut delivered in a military manner—very short, but quickly done.

That evening I went home bracing myself for the usual threats of making me go to a hairstylist the next time, but amazingly, Mrs. Elkmoss said not a word about my hair. The next morning, I got dressed, ate breakfast with the family, and still no mention of my visit to the barber. I do not know if I was thankful for not being berated or disappointed at not being noticed, but off I went to work with still no acknowledgment of my haircut.

I started rounds in the ICU again. By this time my high school patient had been extubated and was alert. Other than some bumps and bruises, he was back to his normal mental status.

"Hello," I began, "you probably don't remember me, but I saw you yesterday morning. You were pretty wiped out. How are you doing today?"

"I'm okay," he said. "I remember you. You've had a haircut since I saw you yesterday."

Both the nurse and I broke out in big smiles as we knew the patient was doing very well. On my way home, though, I realized that my book on women should not include this incident of a nearly comatose teenager being much more observant than a Moss State wife!

CHAPTER 72
REUNIONS

When I received an invitation to attend my thirty-fifth high school reunion, Mrs. Elkmoss was less than enthusiastic. I have to admit that I was not very excited about it either.

I remembered our ten-year reunion. I was a starving third-year medical student and a member of the organization committee was a ward clerk at the University Hospital. One day she asked me if I was planning to attend. She told me that Friday evening of the reunion they would get together at a park near the medical center, and on Saturday evening they would meet at the Moosetown Hotel (the only one in the city). The whole weekend would cost $14 each for a guest and me.

At that time, the only thing harder for me to get than a date was $28. Besides, other than three years in the service, I had been in my hometown going to undergraduate school and then medical school. Since graduating from high school, I had not gotten together with any of my high school classmates. So why should I scrape together a date and money (or was it the other way—money and a date?) to see people I really had not expressed any interest in seeing in all that time?

I did not go to the ten-year reunion, but as the letter about the thirty-fifth sat on my desk for several days, I kept thinking that it might not be such a bad idea. Although it was more expensive than twenty-five years ago, I now had a job and could afford it. Since I was married, it should also be easier to get a date, but convincing Mrs. Elkmoss to attend my high school reunion proved to be a most difficult task.

The reunion gods seemed to favor attending by coincidentally having two of our teenage fawns at summer camps and the third one looking forward to visiting my in-laws. Mrs. Elkmoss was still not convinced, so I came up with a persuasive argument. Supposedly, the high school class celebrating their forty-fifth year reunion was also going to be meeting at the same time. In the back of my mind (later confirmed by several of my demented classmates), I understood that Mr. Famous Actor, one of the very rare people from my high school who made it big, was in that class ten years ahead of us, and we might get a chance to meet him. That was enough to convince the boss to go.

I once read that one of the major causes of weight loss in America is class reunions. I thought it only applied to females, but some strange force took over me. In the course of the six months leading up to the reunion, I lost forty pounds. Mrs. Elkmoss will be quick to point out that I needed to lose fifty, but nonetheless, I was physically fit for the visit with my former colleagues.

The reunion was fun and I had a delightful time meeting with some of my old classmates. I even think Mrs. Elkmoss enjoyed hearing some lies about me. (I did not turn up the heat on our biology teacher's aquarium on the night we left for our senior trip—boiling her fish!) Several folks who had attended previous reunions pointed out that this one was a lot nicer. At the ten-year reunion, everyone was comparing who did what and how much money they made. By the time the thirty-fifth reunion came around, no one cared about such things and just had a good time.

On the final evening, we met in a large ballroom that had been sectioned off to provide for the older class reunion that supposedly had Mr. Famous Actor attending. The plan was that after both reunions were finished with their ceremonies, they would open the sections and share a band for the rest of the evening.

Our side of the ballroom finished first, so Mrs. Elkmoss and I decided to go to the restrooms before the dancing began. The bathrooms were located just outside the entrance to the other ballroom. As I stood there waiting for Mrs. Elkmoss, I could barely hear some of the activities inside. I thought I recognized Famous Actor's voice, so I opened the door a little to look in. Well, it was not the actor I heard, just a geezer from the older class. (It turned out that Famous Actor was actually in the class twelve years ahead of us and he was not within 2,000 miles of our class reunion that night.) I turned around somewhat disappointed, and there was Darlene.

As far as I know, every high school class has a Darlene-type classmate. She was a beautiful cheerleader that eventually married the captain of the football team and never had time for a schmuck like me. That was Darlene. There she was standing in front of me dressed in a slinky black dress, looking almost as thin and beautiful as the day she graduated from high school.

Darlene insisted on giving me a big hug and kiss (this from a girl who hardly spoke to me in high school) and proceeded to tell me about her life, divorce, and present career in Moosetown. Usually (always), I am very dense when it comes to these things, so I miss it when someone makes a pass at me. But I swear (although Mrs. Elkmoss says I was dreaming) my old high school classmate was putting the moves on me.

Just then, the even more beautiful Mrs. Elkmoss returned from the restroom and walked up behind Darlene (although Mrs. Elkmoss denies it) like a female jaguar making sure her kittens were okay. I quickly introduced the two beauties. Darlene was gone in a flash.

It has been several years now since the class reunion. I have gained much of the forty pounds that I lost and Mrs. Elkmoss denies the existence of Darlene. But I still get a great feeling knowing that the most beautiful girl in our high school class made a pass at me.

It gives me incentive to start politicking with my bride to go to the fiftieth reunion. Now that I think about it, it will probably take me that long to convince Mrs. Elkmoss to go.

CHAPTER 73
CREMATION

Mrs. Elkmoss and I have had a long-running discussion (some might say a hostile disagreement) as to whether to be buried in a coffin or just cremated. I highly favor cremation. It seems so much easier and less expensive (I would like to be financially responsible, even in death). It also seems more ecological. There is a certain ravine at our local golf course that has caught many of my golf balls over the years. I maintain if all the golfers who have hit balls there would donate their ashes, we could fill in the ravine. It would leave a wonderful legacy to future players.

Financial and ecological considerations notwithstanding, Mrs. Elkmoss is "dead" set against cremation. She wants a closed coffin, mind you, since she is terrified at the thought of someone actually seeing her lifeless body, but she just does not want to be cremated. She even takes that illogical thought several steps further by advocating that no one else should be cremated.

I have tried to understand the reasons Mrs. Elkmoss has for her feelings about cremation, and I think it goes back to her experience with the ashes of Father and Mother Elkmoss. When Father

Elkmoss died many years ago, he was cremated. Mother Elkmoss was so distraught at the time she could never decide what to do with his ashes and left them at the funeral home. Mother Elkmoss died a dozen years later, a little after I had married Mrs. Elkmoss. Mother Elkmoss was cremated as well and after the memorial service, I went to the funeral home to pick up her ashes. Sister Elkmoss and I had agreed that Mother Elkmoss should probably be buried at the foot of her father's grave where many other Mother Elkmoss's relatives were resting peacefully.

While I was at the funeral home, I asked if they might still have Father Elkmoss's ashes. They did. The box holding the remains was a little dusty but it had the same type of canister as Mother Elkmoss's. Not knowing what to do with the ashes until we could make arrangements to bury them at Mother Elkmoss's family plot (that I had never seen), I took them to the old Elkmoss home and put them on the fireplace mantel while Sister Elkmoss and I tried to settle the estate.

The house sold long before Sister Elkmoss could make arrangements to bury the ashes, so the boxes with the canisters ended up in our garage with a big pile of stuff that represented my half of the estate. Months later when Sister Elkmoss finally made arrangements to bury the ashes, I could not attend. Mrs. Elkmoss was doubly horrified when she found out that the ashes had been sitting in *her* garage for months. It took a long time before she would ever step foot in our garage after that revelation.

You would think that would be the end of that chapter in our lives, but no, Mrs. Elkmoss could not bear to think that I had not seen the gravesite of my parents. There was no easy way to make the daylong trip to the old family plot, but I finally agreed to take our pop-up camper across country to visit with Sister Elkmoss's family. Along the way, we could stop at the gravesite.

The first night's campsite was about an hour away from the graveyard. We planned to eat a leisurely breakfast, visit the family plot, and then drive eight hours more to camp with Sister Elkmoss's family.

While sitting on the step of the camper eating the morning meal, however, I noticed that the tire on that side had lost all its tread and was bald. Fortunately the camper had *a* spare tire (emphasis on "a"). We were a couple of hours behind schedule by the time we got the tire fixed. We then successfully found the cemetery, but I had no idea where the Elkmoss ashes were buried. To make matters worse, the actual plaques for the Elkmoss parents were small and flat. We first had to try to find Mother Elkmoss's mother's maiden name to get to the right family plot.

After an hour of circling around and around in a hot sweaty car with three bored children, I finally convinced Mrs. Elkmoss to get some late lunch. She used that time to call Sister Elkmoss for directions to the gravesite, but she was not home. I wanted to give up at that point, but not Mrs. Elkmoss. She insisted we return and while wandering around the cemetery griping about how late we were going to be in meeting up with Sister Elkmoss. I suddenly heard a loud pop and watched the other tire on the camper go flat.

I efficiently put the bald tire on the camper (after all, I had had a lot of experience by then). We returned to where we ate lunch and called various tire shops to find someone that could fix the flat. Fortunately, there was one tire in the whole town that would fit, and the fellow at the shop agreed to stay past his 5 p.m. closing time. While fixing the tire, Mrs. Elkmoss was finally able to reach my aunt, who was the only other living relative who knew where the family plot was, and got instructions on how to find the burial site.

By that time, there was no way I could have prevented Mrs. Elkmoss from finding the gravesite, so we went back to the cemetery and paid respects to the departed Elkmoss parents. We ended up staying in a motel halfway to the campsite with Sister Elkmoss, but she more than understood our tardiness.

Maybe this explains Mrs. Elkmoss's attitude. I have finally realized that the only way that I will be cremated is to just outlive her.

If I die first, she will do what she wants and I am sure it does not involve cremation. I will be dead, so I will not care. If I survive Mrs. Elkmoss, however, I will still have lots of problems. After living many years with her, I am convinced that she will eventually get her way in this matter, even from the grave.

CHAPTER 74
OBITUARIES

Obituaries, along with tax audits and dentists, are fairly low on my list of interests. I rarely see a humorous one and I certainly have been quite distressed by many. There are three occasions, though, that I have been reminded of the subject. First, when family friends die. Then too, there are some life planning sages that suggest we write down what we would want our obituary to read so we can better plan our lives. Most recently, though, I was confronted with obituaries during research for the history of our medical society. I assumed that was how they would want to be remembered.

Obituaries do not even have to mean someone has died. Take for example the famous mistaken obituary of Mark Twain. At least he had the wit to respond, "The reports of my death are premature." Ernest Hemingway's reported death in an African airplane accident could be excused because of the difficulty of communicating accurately from the bush. It was Alfred Nobel's premature obituary that was probably the most influential, however. Nobel, the inventor of dynamite, was a multimillionaire when his brother died.

Alfred went to attend the funeral and read his brother's obituary. The reporter had mistaken Alfred as being the one who had died and depicted him as the inventor of mass destruction and mayhem. Alfred was so distraught to think that was how people would remember him that he set up and funded one of the most prestigious humanitarian awards in the world—Nobel Prizes.

With that in mind and as a parting shot when I leave our medical society, I have been thinking about some of the things I would want my obituary to include. I certainly would like to be remembered as a person who had a deep love for my country, the medical profession, and most of all, Mrs. Elkmoss and family.

There are other ways to identify one's life and a common one is geographically. I was raised and formally educated in central Moss State. I view that as my true roots. I did my residency in the South, so I really do know what sunshine looks like, but I spent my professional career in Moss State as well.

Another way I could approach my obituary is in terms of people who had contributed to the richness and fullness of my life. This includes a grandfather who always kept pennies in a little wicker basket on his refrigerator and split them up with his grandchildren when they visited. The memories also include a grandmother whose lap was the most comfortable place in the world. As grandchildren we would always vie for it when we would ride with her in a car. Father Elkmoss taught me to "study and prepare yourself, and one day your opportunity will come." Mother Elkmoss, after raising a family, struggled not only to complete her interrupted bachelor's degree, but finished a master's degree, underscoring the importance of learning.

Those people are also dead, but I would want my obituary to emphasize those people living who helped shape my life. My family, many teachers, coaches, ministers, colleagues, and friends that contributed to who I am are countless, but nonetheless vital.

In reality, obituaries are for the living, not the dead, so perhaps my reluctance to dwell on the subject is a little unfounded. I am still having trouble figuring out how my obituary will help me plan my life, but hopefully I will have a long time, while avoiding dentists and tax audits, to work on it.